BECAUSE
I CAN

NEW YORK TIMES BESTSELLING AUTHOR
LISA RENEE JONES

ISBN-13: 979-8795503288

CHAPTER ONE

Once the lights go out upstairs, I know I'm not crazy. Someone is in the house.

Huddled in the dark corner of the wine cellar of the house Tyler inherited from his grandmother, the home I'm presently living in, I listen for any and all sounds, praying whoever is here will just go away. I've given up on the call to 911 actually connecting and I can only pray that when Dash and I were disconnected, he called them for me. Seconds tick by like hours and there is nothing happening. I begin to explain away what is happening.

Could the other Allison be in the house? Maybe it's her and she has no idea there's another tenant? Who else has the alarm code but her? Tyler, I think. Natalie from Human Resources, as well. I should have changed it. Why didn't I change it?

More time passes, and then suddenly rapid, heavy footsteps sound above. My heart thunders in my chest before I hear, "Allie!"

At the sound of Dash's voice, I'm on my feet screaming, "Dash! Dash! Down here." The lights are on again above.

I'm already running up the stairs when he appears at the top in the doorway. Relief, so much relief, floods my body, at the sight of him. He catches me as I clear the last step and pulls me into his arms. "Are you okay?" he demands urgently, scooping me close. "Are you okay?"

"Now I am," I say, clinging to the T-shirt he's wearing, and swallowing hard with the sight of his black eye and swollen face. "God," I whisper, touching his jaw. "Dash."

He catches my hand, ignoring my concern for his own. "You scared the fuck out of me, Allie."

As he did me, I think, flashing back to him in that underground club, about him daring the other fighter to hit him, *wanting* him to hit him. Wanting me to go away and just let him self-destruct, when that was never going to happen. But he's here now. He came for me when I wasn't sure he would, not after what I witnessed in that underground club.

"Not intentionally," I say. "Dash I—I didn't think you'd come."

Footsteps sound, and already on edge, I jerk around to find a tall, dark-haired man wearing jeans and a T-shirt approaching. "All clear," he announces, holstering his weapon.

Dash's hand is on my shoulder. "Easy, baby. He's a friend."

Baby.

As if were still together. As if I'm still in his life.

"Thanks, Jack," Dash says, releasing me to shake his hand. "I owe you. Come drive the M4. Hell, I'll give you the damn thing."

It hits me then that this is the cop who pulled Dash over that first night we were together. Jack chuckles. "I won't hold you to that, man. Just happy I was nearby," he adds, glancing at me. "You okay ma'am?"

"I am," I say. "Thank you for coming. I swear I set the alarm. I don't know how anyone got in here, but someone *was* here. I heard them walking around. They turned out the light."

"I checked the alarm," Jack says. "It's off. If someone was here, they had the code. Who would that be?"

Dash's jaw sets hard, and I know immediately where his head is at. "It wasn't Tyler." I glance at Jack. "That's my landlord," I explain. "He wasn't here. I talked to him.

It could have been the woman who lived here before me. She had a personal relationship with my landlord. I'm not sure she knew someone else moved in."

"Then why run off when we arrived?" Jack asks, obviously not buying that idea.

My cellphone rings in my hand, and I know with dread in my belly and without even looking at caller ID that it's going to be Tyler. Sure enough, it's Tyler, and considering the circumstances, there's really no way to avoid him right now. I glance at the other two men. "It's my landlord." My gaze goes to Dash. "I called him to see if he was here and then hung up on him. I need to—"

"Take the call."

The command is short, biting, and feels like a slammed door between us, a reminder of what I walked into tonight at that fight ring, and who lead me there. Tyler might have had good intentions, for at least part of this night, but he instigated trouble. Unable to win or fight this moment, I answer the line, "Tyler."

"What the hell?" he demands. "I tried to call you back ten fucking times. I called the police."

"So did Dash," I say quickly. "And they're here."

"As in the police or the police and Dash?"

"Both," I say, as Jack asks, "Can I talk to him?"

"One of the officers wants to talk to you, Tyler," I say. "Can I put him on?"

"I'm almost there, but yes, put him on."

Wonderful. He's almost here. This night just won't stop giving. "Don't," I say, hoping he reads between the lines, hoping he's smart enough to know that he and Dash, together tonight is the hornet's nest of all hornet's nest. "But here is the officer." I hand the phone to Jack while my gaze collides with Dash's.

Jack begins talking to Tyler while Dash and I just stare at each other, his eyes narrowing on mine, understanding in their depths. He knows I told Tyler to stay away. I'm glad he knows. After a night fighting over Tyler, Dash needs to know I chose him as if that was ever even up for discussion. *Of course*, I chose him.

But despite my intended message, the pulse in Dash's jaw says he is not pleased, and I get it, I do. Tyler insinuated himself into Dash's life tonight, and me with him, in a way Dash had not yet intended, and may never have allowed, which was intrusive. He stole Dash's freedom to choose and exposed his dirty secret. But on the flip side of the coin, Tyler wasn't wrong to be worried about him. And I can't regret knowing what I now know, not if I can help Dash. I just really hate the way this all came about.

But the universe works in mysterious ways and Dash needed an intervention.

I know that now, standing here with Dash, looking at the damage to his face. That doesn't mean Tyler is forgiven or welcomed either. He needs to stay away right now. He needs to give Dash space. He needs to give me a chance to protect him, to help him. To just be with him.

Seconds have ticked by like hours when Jack finally hands me the phone. "He wants to talk to you."

He being Tyler again, of course, and I accept the phone while Jack eyes Dash. "I'm going to look around out back. You two stay here in the kitchen until I give you the 'all clear.'"

"Thank you," I say, but Jack is already heading toward the door.

I press the phone to my ear and say, "Tyler?"

Dash's expression tightens, almost as if he can't even stand Tyler's name on my lips. So much so that he turns away, walking to the kitchen, his back to me, as he presses his hands onto the island, his shoulders bunched.

"Are you sure someone was in the house?" Tyler asks. "Someone was here," I assure him. "The lights were on and they went out." As if reacting to news he's already heard, but perhaps digests differently or fully now, Dash turns to face me again as I add, "I know I turned on the alarm, but it's off now. Could it have been Allison?"

There's a several-beat pause before Tyler says, "I don't know. Maybe. I'm trying to reach her. If I hear anything I'll call you." He hesitates. "I wasn't wrong tonight. Talk sense into him or I will before he self-destructs."

My agitation with Tyler is real. He pushed Dash tonight and he knew what he was doing. Or perhaps he didn't expect to push Dash as far as he did. I don't know what to think at this point.

I slide my phone into the pocket of my jeans. Dash catches my hand and walks me to him, the heat in our touch as addictive as I fear it is radioactive. We're still all taut anger and attraction, mixed together in combustible heat. His fingers slide under my hair and he drags my mouth to his. There's a pulse between us and then he's kissing me, a deep, demanding, angry kiss before he says, "You aren't staying here. You're coming home with me."

I could tell him that we can't pretend tonight didn't happen. I could remind him that we just talked about me moving in with him, and recap all the reasons I said no. I could tell him that when I saw the Russian Beast beating on him, the idea of him being hurt, destroyed me.

There are so many things I could say, but right now, in this volatile state that defines us, I decide that less is more. "Yes." That is all I say. Just yes.

"Can I have a word, Dash?"

At the sound of Jack's voice, Dash strokes my hair. "Go pack."

"I already have my things at your place. I really don't need anything."

He turns me toward the bedroom. "Take more," he orders softly, which could mean he still wants me to live with him, or maybe he just wants to get rid of me to talk to Jack. The reality here is that after tonight, I don't know where we stand, what he wants, or even what I want.

For now, a reprieve is welcomed and the truth is, I do need to pack. I quit my job and I'll have to move anyway. I don't know what that means for the charity event or my involvement, but I know that my working for Tyler is causing trouble. Ironically, I think as I step into the bathroom, I've blamed myself for tonight, but at the root of every problem, was Tyler. He showed up at the bar tonight. He picked a fight with Dash. He was what triggered me and Dash fighting.

I grab a bag from the closet and start filling it, a bit sad that my new house is already my old house, but it's not really about the house as much as it is yet another shift in my life. I don't know where I'm going or what I'm doing, but if I'm honest with myself, that reaches well beyond one night. I need to dig my feet in and be emotionally brave enough to really face my future, which means facing my past. Just not tonight.

I open a drawer and there sits the necklace box, at least one connection between my life and Allison's in one place. She left her career behind, perhaps more. But did she really walk away, or did she walk forward to something better?

I pick up the box and lift the lid, staring down at the gorgeous stones.

"You're obsessed with that necklace," Dash says from the doorway.

I shut the lid and turn back to face him. "It's thousands of dollars. What if someone came for it, not me, tonight?"

"That sounds like a good reason to get you out of here."

"There are cameras," I remember. "We should be able to see who was here on the cameras."

"They were off," he announces. "Jack checked."

My brows dip. "What do you mean *off*? The cameras work even when the security system is off."

"I mean they were working up until tonight and somehow they were just flipped off."

I curl forward, hugging myself. "What is this Dash?"

He catches my waist and walks me to him, "I just want you out of here."

I don't argue. I'm suddenly more eager than ever to leave this house and not come back.

LISA RENEE JONES

CHAPTER TWO

The problem with the unknown is its haunting ability to know what you do not. It's such a silly wordplay I know, but it's also the truth. The unknown is the monster that wants to remain unknown, and it drives us crazy. Dash hangs out while I pack, hovering nearby as if he feels the presence of that monster and fears I may be snatched out of his reach any moment.

For me, that monster is the necklace and yet, I'm going to take it with me, rather than leave it behind.

I retrieve it from the bathroom counter, grab it and stick it in one of my overnight bags. Dash manages to appear in the doorway at just that moment. "Before you say I'm obsessed with it again, I don't know what to do with it," I say. "And it's too expensive for me to just leave behind, especially when it's a compelling reason to break into the house in the first place."

"Carrying it around isn't the answer," he says, obviously referencing the way I'd had it with me when I'd had drinks with Tyler and his father, whose name is ironically, considering the officer's name helping us tonight, Jack. The necklace had fallen out of my purse and ultimately Tyler had learned that it was Allison's, a gift from another man. I guess on some level he didn't want to believe there was someone else in her life.

"We'll start by locking it in my safe," Dash suggests, snapping me out of my reverie. "And you in my apartment."

"You're going to lock me in your apartment?" I challenge.

He catches my hips, his touch possessive as he walks me to him. "Yes. If that's what it takes to protect you."

There's a dark pulse between us that radiates with every moment that went oh so terribly wrong tonight. He says he wants to protect me and that feels kind of nice, but I'm not the only one that needs protection. He does, too. My hands go to his wrist. "Will you be with me?"

"I shouldn't have let you leave in the first place. I shouldn't have walked away when I did. Then none of this would have happened."

None of *this*.

Three extremely simple and yet complicated words, too much to even touch right now. "Should we talk to Jack about the necklace?"

"There's a lot about tonight, neither of us understands," he says. "Let's figure out our own questions and answers before we go creating new problems."

In other words, he's not sure Tyler doesn't have everything to do with everything that happened tonight. And the thing is, I'm not sure I can argue otherwise, but what I can't do is ignore how ever-present, and yet absent, Allison is in every moment of my life. "I'm starting to worry about Allison, Dash. Should I be worried?"

His jaw flexes. "What did Tyler say?"

"He's trying to reach her."

"He might not be the one to actually get her to respond." There's disapproval in his tone that speaks of the two men's history, and I'm reminded of Tyler's insistence that Dash is not only bad for me, but Dash knows that as a fact. But there was also a reference to Dash warning Tyler away from another woman.

Allison, I wonder?

BECAUSE I CAN

It's a question for later, not now. "I've tried to reach her as well," I say. "That's why I worry we need to talk to Jack."

"We'll have Jack reach out to her."

"Thank you, Dash. I'm sure my worries for Allison are unfounded, but I can't say they don't exist anymore. They do."

"She left, Allie. Just like you left publishing. Everything different isn't bad."

He's right, of course. Logically I know this, but my gut isn't about logic. It's about something that cannot be seen or spoken. It's just there, demanding attention. Needing to hear something to shut it up I say, "And you think that was better for her." It's not really a question considering his obvious feelings, and yet, I need an answer.

His cellphone rings and his lips press together. "Almost as if the universe doesn't want me to go there." He snakes his phone from his pocket. "My sister."

"She probably heard there was an issue at the bar."

"Or Tyler called her."

"He didn't. He told me you wouldn't want him to call her."

His lips press together, his eyes shuttering, as he answers his phone, turning away from me as he does. And I fear that is exactly where we are headed—me standing right in front of him and him turning away.

LISA RENEE JONES

CHAPTER THREE

The idea that Allison was here, rather than someone else, settles into my gut and wants to hang out, but it's also far more appealing an idea than an intruder.

As I watch Jack and a group of officers investigate my break-in, I decide Dash was right about leaving the necklace out of tonight's equation. I mean technically, it feels a bit like I'm the one who stole it, and the more that idea takes root, the more awkward and wrong it feels. I have to do something to return the necklace to the sender and pretty darn quickly.

When all that can be done in the wee hours of the morning has been done, Jack gives us one last update, and then he's gone. Dash loads my bags into his trunk and then helps me into the passenger side of the M4, kneeling beside me as he does. He reaches over me, his body warm, as he slides my belt into place. "I was already on my way to see you when you called." His fingers brush my jaw. "And thank fuck I was. You have no idea how freaked out I was when your call dropped."

"And you have no idea how relieved I was to hear your voice." I touch his face.

A mix of heat and emotion pulses between us, seconds ticking by, but there's nothing more to say. Not now. Not like this. Maybe not even tonight or should I say, this morning? There have been too many harsh words, too many words laden with booze, too many, so many.

Dash pushes to his feet and seals me inside the car. A minute later, he slides into the car beside me and I'm still reeling from his words. He was on his way to me when I called. I guess on some level I knew this.

Otherwise, he wouldn't have made it to me so quickly after the phone call, but hearing him say it, hits me in a whole different way. Despite everything that happened tonight, first, he's concerned I was really in danger tonight, and I wonder what he knows that I don't know, but even more so, I needed Dash and he was here for me. For now, that's where I want to root myself, where I want to root us and with good reason. My mind goes to him in that ring, allowing that man to beat on him, even daring him to hurt him. I squeeze my eyes shut with the visual, the *horrible* visual.

Dash needs me, too, I think.

He says he should never have left me tonight. I should never have left him.

We are, without any doubt, two messed up people, both of us spiraling out of control, in our own way. The question becomes, do we land more gently together, or do we accelerate the inevitable crash and burn? I don't know the answer, but he wasn't better without me tonight and I wasn't better without him either. I sink down lower into my seat, settling into the idea of what is right tonight, me here with Dash. The warm heat of the car and the lethargy of too much booze and not enough sleep are ever-present, but I fight the heaviness of my lashes, rotating to my side to face Dash.

He glances over at me and catches my hand, and it feels like everything that was wrong is right. That's the lie I tell myself, but it's a good lie. One I'd like to pretend isn't a lie for the rest of the night. Just tonight. That's all I want. And I think it's what Dash wants as well. Tomorrow is another day, one we will face with a bright light that will scorch us with the burn of reality. But that's then. And this is now.

CHAPTER FOUR

The calm beneath the storm is locked in a fragile silence.

Dash and I don't speak on the short ride to his apartment and not for a lack of words. I haven't even asked him about the call with his sister, let alone, the ten other questions that come to my mind about Tyler, Allison, and of course, his fighting habit. But Dash knows we have to talk. Pushing him, and making that happen now, rather than later, could ultimately push him over the edge. And I'm not sure just how dangerous that edge might be, not after what I saw tonight.

Once we arrive at the apartment, Dash doesn't pull us to the front of the building, but enters the private garage. I can't help but wonder if that has something to do with his bruised and abused face or maybe it's just how bruised the two of us are together. Dash parks in a private space, kills the engine, and when I'm planning to exit my side of the vehicle to meet him, he's already there, opening my door and helping me to my feet. His eye is swollen now, so very swollen, and while I have no doubt his body is all about pain and punishment, both of which he'd welcomed, it's my heart that hurts, and it hurts for him. Tyler isn't wrong when he says Dash is punishing himself. And what kind of pain must Dash feel, to want to do this to himself?

"This is where you belong," he says softly. "With me."

My aching heart races with this declaration made more impactful by the fact that I saw behind the veil tonight. I know his secret or at least part of his secret, and he still wants me with him. I also know that he doesn't share his secrets with anyone, not intentionally, not even me. But he's also not running away. In other words, Dash is far braver than I have been in my life. He faces his problems, even if he does so in a self-destructive way. But is it really more self-destructive than running and hiding?

And I do run.

I ran away from him earlier. In truth, I've run away from a lot in my life, too much, it seems. But that ends now and with that decision, and despite the fact that deep down, I know that Dash will eventually leave me bleeding and heartbroken, every reservation I'd had about staying with him until I leave in January, falls away.

"I should never have left, Dash. I really, really wish I could turn back time and do this night over again."

"You're not the one who messed this night up. I am. It's all on me."

Tyler's reference to Dash's fighting habit since his brother's death hits home in this moment. While I don't know the details of that tragedy, in my core, I believe that Dash owning too much blame in his life is why he ever stepped into a fight ring. "We both made mistakes tonight," I say. "*I made* mistakes tonight. I own those mistakes. Leaving was one of them."

His fingers flex on my hips, his eyes flickering with some emotion that I cannot name but I can feel the tug between us, the bond, growing in that moment. He needs to know that I want to be here. And I believe, too, that he needs to know that I'm not judging him. I hope that's what he now knows, but I'm going to drive home the point, every chance I am gifted.

"Let's go upstairs," he urges softly.

"Yes," I agree. "Yes, please."

Dash releases me and pops the trunk, removing my bags before we head to the elevator. Once we're inside the main elevator, on the move, there's this odd mix of comfort and discomfort between me and Dash that drives me nuts. I want us to be back to normal. I want this night to never have happened. But it did. Tyler ripped open the door to Dash's torment tonight and welcomed me to step inside. Now, I'm there, living in a space Dash didn't invite me to visit. And while he's clearly not pushing me out of that space, we are in uncharted territory. We don't know how to live together in this new reality.

At Dash's door, he sets my bags down, unlocks the door, and then pushes it open, motioning me forward. It's a gentlemanly act, allowing my early entry, but it's more than that right now. Everything between me and Dash is a question that leads to another question. Do I really want to be here? Am I going to live here? He grabs my bags again and now that his hands are occupied, I step in front of him, hands on his chest, and lean into him. With his hard chest beneath my hands, I push to my toes and kiss him. It's a fast kiss, but it's all me. I instigate it, I make it happen, and I do so with a message that is about commitment, me to him. I'm not here because I have to be, it's a choice and I choose here and him. A message I follow up by walking inside the apartment. And maybe, just maybe, if we can work it out, my apartment as well as his for a few short months.

Until I leave.

Just the idea guts me, it really does, and it hits me that I quit my job here. I made sure that staying isn't a financial option. But me in the middle of Tyler and Dash seems a problem as well. It's a problem I'll have to face and soon. Just not tonight.

Tonight is all about me and Dash crashing into each other.

And about me praying that crash doesn't come with a burn. At least not an immediate burn.

CHAPTER FIVE

Dash joins me inside the apartment and lifts his chin toward the bedroom.

We head in that direction, but I'm not thinking about seduction. I'm thinking about how much he needs ice on that eye, and how much my gut tells me not to bring attention to it right now.

Once we're at the bedroom door, Dash flips on the light and then the fireplace. "I need to wash this night off of me," he says. "I'll put your bags in the closet."

He's already walking away, leaving me to decide what I do next. It doesn't feel like he's telling me he needs to be alone. Not at all, but it does feel like another question, though I don't really understand the context. But he needs me and I came here to be with him. And truly, maybe, I'm reading too much into everything. Maybe, just maybe, he assumed I'd follow him. If so, he's right.

That's exactly what I do. I follow him.

I'm in the hallway when the shower turns on. I arrive in the bathroom doorway as Dash tugs his shirt over his head, and does so with a grunt. I cringe at the sight of the dark bruises down his right side. His body is strong but I know now that so is his self-hate. Dash *hates* himself and that's a brutal reality that cannot be denied. Not by me and not by him.

I want to know why, but I'm all too aware of the fact that I won't find that answer in a simple spoken word. That's exactly why I don't ask questions, and I don't cross to him and offer lame comfort that will do nothing but drive him away. I'm all about washing the dirt of this night off and doing so with him, not without him, which is almost where this night had me landing. God, how I wish we could just wash it all away and leave us with nothing but my version of sunshine: lemon drops, dancing with Dash, hot sex, and the waffles his sister and my mother makes for us.

But it's not that simple. It was never going to be simple at all.

I reach for the zipper of my skirt. He reaches for his jeans. And together, we undress, watching each other as we do so, the absence of words, offering the freedom for us to live in the moment and each other. When the layers of clothing are gone, only our secrets between us, he catches my hand and walks me to him, the thickness of his erection at my hip. The heat of his hard body aligned with mine. The intensity of his stare, sheltered by hooded eyes. He doesn't break the sanctuary of our silence. He doesn't kiss me. He simply leads me into the shower where the steam has gathered and offered us a safe haven.

Dash and I stand under the warm water, and just as he said, we let the water wash away the dirt of a dirty night. I grab the soap and drizzle it on his chest, but when I run my hand over the area, he flinches. My breath catches with his reaction, with the certainty that he is more badly beaten than I'd realized, and I'd already known he was not in good condition.

Before I can stop myself, I break the silence. "Dash—"

That's all it takes. He captures my head and damp hair in his hand, an erotic pull that ensures I won't ask a question, I won't demand answers. But he demands, oh how he demands. His mouth crashes down over mine and he doesn't just kiss me. He consumes me, breathes me in, *owns* me. I'm panting when he presses me against the wall. I'm gasping as he lifts my leg and presses the hard length of his cock against me. I'm clinging to him as he presses inside me and drives deep. For a few beats, we're just there, our bodies joined, our breaths heavy, a mix of passion and emotion between us.

One of his hands scoops my backside, arching my hips, and dragging him deeper. The other hand finds my breast, his fingers dragging over my nipple before he's tugging on it with a pinching pain that clenches my sex. And then he's thrusting into me, pumping hard and fast, his gaze raking over my bouncing breasts, a wild frenzy erupting between us. I hold onto him anywhere I can manage to touch him, as if I will never touch him again. And he touches me with just as much desperation. As if he feared he'd never touch me again.

Urgency roars between us, hot with demand and need.

Dash scoops my backside with powerful hands and lifts me. My legs instinctively wrap around his waist. He shifts me into the corner, anchors me, and then he's driving into me. Over and over, sensations explode through me. In between his powerful thrusts, his mouth is on my mouth, his tongue against my tongue. Every emotion, good and bad, that this night has created, I feel in his touch, his kiss, the pump of our bodies. The build of pleasure is sharp and fierce and I try to push it back, to hold back, to make this last, but Dash is so incredibly hard, his face contorted in wicked passion, his muscles flexing with such beauty, and I just can't. I shatter, my sex clenching around him, and Dash groans with the impact. He pumps against my spams, and throws his head back, quaking with his own release.

When it's over, we're back to burying the storm in the silence. We shower together, soaping each other, touching each other, but we don't speak. When the water runs cold and Dash turns it off, we end up in bed, in the dark, holding each other. I shut my eyes reminding myself that no matter how good this bed that is my bed with Dash feels, there will be a last night. And it won't be that far away. I cannot lose perspective or I'll be the one who ends up badly beaten, only my pain will be emotional, not physical.

CHAPTER SIX

I wake to rain pitter-pattering on the window pane, laying on my side, with Dash wrapped around me from behind. I have about thirty seconds to appreciate this cozy moment before I realize that the doorbell is ringing. "Dash?" I murmur. "Dash, the doorbell—"

"Ignore it."

The prior night comes crashing back and I'm instantly thinking of Allison, Tyler, the police, and more. "What if it's important?"

"It's my sister, Allie. I'm not talking to her this morning."

His cellphone starts ringing on the nightstand. He doesn't move. And I can't move because he's holding onto me. Which isn't going to work. I know he knows it's not going to work.

"I don't know Bella well yet, Dash, but I know her well enough to know she's not going to go away."

His cellphone goes silent and starts to ring again almost instantly. He curses and rolls away from me, planting himself on his back, his arms to his side. I shift to face him and gasp at the sight of his swollen eye. "Oh my God, Dash. Your eye. It's so bad."

"Which is why I can't see my sister right now."

"Right," I say, realization and understanding overtaking me. I shift to my knees, one of Dash's T-shirts covering my body, my mind kicking into problem-solving mode. "Okay. Let's think this through. She's here so we can't leave her outside the door. I can go and talk to her."

He sits up. "And tell her what? She'll come up here to see me, Allie. And she'll freak the fuck out."

25

His phone is ringing again. Mine will be next. I know this. He has to know this, too, and my mind races with a way to get us out of this. "Did you have a breakfast date with her today?"

"No, but she randomly stops in."

"We could tell her we're at my parent's place and your phone was in the car and now my mother won't stop talking. You could text her."

His jaw flexes. "I hate lying to her and she'll just come by later." He glances at me, and I can barely see his eye. "And this is going to take at least ten days to heal."

"Then we take this head-on. You were with me last night. Tell her you got in a fight, which is not a lie. Outside the bar, which technically is also true as well. You weren't in the bar. And she won't believe you were at the underground ring when you were with me."

"She'll *know*, Allie. She knows enough to read between the lines and it won't be okay to her."

"You have me by your side on this, Dash." His phone is ringing again. "Tell her to come in. We'll be down in ten minutes."

His lips press together but he grabs his phone and answers with, "Can't a man sleep late?" Obviously, she says something in reply as he answers with, "Yeah, well, I'm feeling like shit. Let yourself in. We'll be down in a minute." He disconnects and looks at me. "I was going to have to deal with this with her, but leave it to my sister to make me do it now." He throws away the blanket and stands up. "And without a damn shower. I'm going to brush my teeth and wash my face."

His tone is cranky for sure, but I know he's bruised, beaten, and hurting. And on some level, on perhaps a wildly evident level, I keep going back to Tyler being an asshole, but he wasn't wrong when he said that Dash believes he deserves to be punished. Maybe this, what is happening this morning with his sister, is even a part of his punishment, something he feels he deserves, even if this part of the equation would be avoided if possible.

Interesting though, people with bad habits, know how to hide them. The very fact that he's not prepared to hide this from her, has me wondering if he really hasn't fought in years, or if he somehow avoids his sister by design, at designated times?

Dash stalks toward the bathroom. I'm still standing in the same spot when the alarm on the front door sounds, and Bella is officially in the apartment. This means I need to pull myself together and look presentable enough to be comfortable navigating a whole lot of potential sibling trouble. I rush after Dash, find him at the bathroom sink, and join him, to do exactly what he's doing, brush my teeth.

Once we're both holding brushes, this becomes a shared, intimate, domestic moment, that does funny things to my belly. When our eyes meet in the mirror, there's a punch of awareness between us. But there's also his damaged face and the dread that is not only his, but mine, over Bella's reaction.

"She's going to freak out," I say softly.

"I know," he replies. "Believe me, I know." The grimness of his tone tells me that, yes, this is punishment. But not the kind he welcomes.

He pushes off the sink and exits to the hallway and the closets. I fight the urge to follow and press him to talk to me, recognizing that he's a man of control that's had control stripped away from him. We haven't even faced this situation, and now, he's facing me and Bella, in one swift hellish morning. He needs space to pull himself together. I grab one of my bags that's thankfully already in the bathroom and start pulling out the items that I need to try to make my hair and face respectable. Since I cried hard last night, I'm all puffed up and I don't want Bella to ask questions that only lead to lies. And my hair, my God my hair, is a mess. It dried naturally only a few hours ago, and it dried looking like I stuck my finger in a socket. It's a disaster. Digging in to fix the mess I am, I grab my flat iron from my bag and plug it up. A few minutes later, I've tamed the mess on my head, used stringent pads, moisturizer, and applied a little makeup and lip gloss. At this point, I look tired, not hungover from tears. I think. I hope.

I hurry into the closet, pull on leggings, a sweater, and sneakers, eager to join Dash. I find him at the window, dressed in jeans and a T-shirt, with boots, his hand on the glass. As if he senses my presence, he turns to face me. And in the sunlight, that shiner is shining all right.

"I think I should go talk to Bella. Just wait here." I round the coffee table and wrap my arms around him. "Really, Dash. It's bad. Seeing her later, not sooner, when it's not this dramatically horrid is a good idea."

"You can't save me from my sister, cupcake."

"I don't want to save you from Bella. I just want to soften the impact of her reaction. Don't underestimate me. I can do more to help than you think I can."

"I assure you, Allie, I do *not* underestimate you on this or anything else. But neither do I underestimate my sister's reaction. Let her scream and shout because she will. And then let this be over." He catches my arms and pulls me to him. "I know we have to talk, but when we get down there—"

"I'm with you, Dash," I say, meaning it in every possible way. "I told you. I shouldn't have left last night. Nothing that happened after I did changes that."

"It depends on what changed your mind."

28

"You," I say. "You changed my mind."

"I'm not good for you, Allie. I know that. And I know what the right thing to do is."

"What does that mean, Dash?"

"*It means,* I know what I should do right now, but I'm just not going to do it."

My stomach knots. Is he talking about walking away from me? Or continuing to fight? "*What* does that mean?"

"Dash!"

At the sound of Bella's voice from somewhere nearby, Dash's jaw clenches. "If we don't go to her, she'll come to us. We deal with her. Then we'll deal with everyone else."

Only I'm not sure we will. I'm not sure of much right now. I don't know where Allison is. I don't know who was in my house last night. I don't know why Dash is punishing himself. I don't know what to do about any of it.

CHAPTER SEVEN

The minute Bella's gaze lands on Dash she gasps, her hand covering her mouth, her eyes shutting. "God, no," she whispers, and then when I expect her to lose it and freak out on Dash, she does just the opposite. She does what I don't expect.

She rushes to Dash and wraps her arms around him, hugging him with all her might, her head pressed to his chest. For my part, my attention is on Dash's tormented expression, and the slow fold of his arms as they close around her. The instant he hugs her, her chin tilts upward, her gaze seeking his. "Why?" she asks softly. "Why now? Things are so good for you, Dash."

Pain stabs through me at Dash's situation and without even thinking, I rush to his rescue. "Someone broke into my house last night. Dash saved me."

"Oh my God," Bella murmurs, pulling away from Dash, her attention sliding between us. "Broke in? While you were there?"

"Exactly," I explain, leaving out the part where I was alone, and Dash was not there. "Thank God for Dash. He ended up fighting some big monster of a man, and all because of me," I add because it's how I honestly feel. He was fighting last night because I left him. And he did fight a monster of a man. That monster was in a fight club, not at my house, but Bella doesn't need to know that.

I can feel Dash's eyes on me but I stay focused on Bella as I continue with, "I don't know who he was or how this happened."

"Oh my God," she gasps again, but this time it's different, the complicated fear of Dash fighting again is

31

gone. "This is so scary," she continues. "What if Dash hadn't shown up? Was it a break-in? Did they think the house was vacant?"

"I don't know what it was," I say. "The other Allison lived in that house not long ago. Maybe someone was looking for her. Maybe the man came with her and she didn't know I'd taken over the house."

She blinks. "Wait. What? You're in the same house Allison was in? How is that possible?"

"I think I need coffee to tell this story," I say, glancing at Dash. "And you need ice or heat or both on that eye."

"Both," Bella declares. "He needs to do both. I'll get a pack of ice together and I already made coffee." She wags a finger between us. "Both of you. Go sit at the bar. I brought bagels and cream cheese. You both need to eat. And I'll pour you coffee." She turns and rushes toward the island.

Dash catches my hand and pulls me in front of him, leaning down to press his lips to my ear. "Thank you. And you didn't make me do anything, Allie. I own this. Just me." He pulls back to look at me. "Understand?"

"It's not that simple, now is it?"

"Come you two love birds. Coffee. Food. Me."

At Bella's teasing prod Dash's lips press together, but he swings me around and under his arm as he guides me to do as commanded. Dash and I each claim a barstool and steamy cups of coffee are already in front of us. Bella then sets a bundle of ice next to Dash. "You look like you ran into my doorknob again."

Dash laughs, and glances over at me. "I was chasing her when we were kids. She tried to slam the door in front of me. I managed to take the knob in my face. And yes, I was short, but not that short. Apparently, I bent over." He grimaces at Bella. "And I was the one who got grounded."

BECAUSE I CAN

"Because you broke mom's vase," she objects, "not because you took a doorknob in the eye. And you were babysitting. Mom was fair on all things. You know that."

He grunts and shoves the ice on his face. The toaster pops and she turns around and attends to the food. I glance over at Dash. "Don't you need to work on your book today?"

"Don't remind me. My head is pounding and it does me no good to write a bunch of garbage."

It's more than his head. He needs to be in a hot tub of water, soaking out the aches and pains, and he will be, as soon as Bella leaves. I'll make sure of it.

Bella sets a plate in front of each of us, both with cream cheese-covered bagels on top. "I have Advil in my purse. I'll get you some." She pushes off the island and heads into the living area, where she obviously set her purse.

Dash sets the ice down and glances over at me, his lips pressed together. "You're right. I have to get words on the page. My own stupidity is no excuse for not doing my job."

"Your own stupidity?" Bella asks, reappearing way too quickly with a bottle in her hand. "What does that mean, Dash?" She's scowling again, suspicion in her tone as she sets the Advil in front of him.

"It means, I thought I could actually make that early deadline you wanted. Now I went off and got the shit beat out of me like a little pussy, and I'm no longer in that same head space."

Oh, he's good. He just moved the conversation from her suspicion to what matters to her—him and his work-in-progress. And as he knew she would, she peps up. "You think you might make an earlier deadline?"

"If you stop drilling me and let me go sleep a couple of hours and get to work. Maybe."

33

Correction, he's not just good, he's sensational. He didn't just redirect her attention from his black eye, he gave her a reason to leave and stop drilling him.

"Don't get my hopes up for nothing, Dash."

"I'm not getting your hopes up at all," he says, downing the Advil with a gulp of coffee. "I'm saying I'm trying. That's more than I said before." He motions to me. "And you can thank Allie for that. She made me read the book from the beginning. I decided it doesn't suck as badly as I thought."

"It doesn't suck at all," I chime in. "It's brilliant."

"Really?" she asks. "I mean, of course, it is. It's Dash we're talking about here." She glances at him. "And you and your brilliance have a charity event signing in two weeks. Are you going to be ready?"

"If you go home and let me sleep this off."

"Sleeping doesn't heal black eyes."

"Sleep heals," he argues. "So does silence." He grinds his teeth, but not because of Bella. "My damn head feels like a drank a bottle of tequila and didn't have the fun that goes along with it," he grumbles.

"Eat," she orders. "You know you get headaches when you don't eat."

"That's you not me," he reminds her.

"Right. Well, you still need to eat. And I need coffee." She turns around and grabs a cup from the cabinet and fills one for herself. I love how at home she is in Dash's place. I love what that says about their relationship and about Dash as a man.

I glance at Dash, but his discomfort is palpable, and rather than look at me, he reaches for his bagel. He's a mess because a) I've pierced the veil of his second life, and b) he really doesn't like to lie to Bella, and avoiding those lies right now feels a bit like we're flies dodging a fly swatter. He would do anything for Bella. And his torment over keeping things from her, speaks of a flawed man who can still love everyone but himself, and I swear in this realization I find I fall harder for him than ever.

I don't know what is behind Dash's pain, not fully, maybe not at all, and I wonder if Bella knows, either. The only thing I do know is that Dash can't go on like this. He has a battle to fight for himself and I'm determined to make him see that he's worth that fight.

CHAPTER EIGHT

Bella busies about the kitchen while Dash is hyper-focused on his plate, his gaze downturned and not by accident.

The eyes are the window to the soul.

And while that might be true, I believe most of us are shuttered, protecting ourselves from vulnerability. I don't believe I ever looked into Brandon's eyes and saw his soul, or I would have seen the poison thriving inside him. Dash wears a façade of this easy-going guy who gets along with most everyone, Tyler excluded, of course, when the truth is, deep inside he's all pain and torment. No one sees the truth of who he is because he doesn't want them to see those things.

And yet, I did.

And I do.

And I know that right now, he's just trying to get through this encounter with his sister without it exploding in his face while expecting a similar situation with me later today. I don't want him to dread the conversation with me. The minute I have the chance, I'll make sure he knows that while I want to know him and understand why he fights, I won't demand answers.

Bella rejoins us at the island with her coffee in hand. Eager to please her, and thus keep her mind off Dash's injuries, I quickly bite into what proves to be a delicious chocolate chip bagel with cream cheese. "These are wonderful, and a bit sinful, I do believe," I say, offering my eager approval, as she claims the seat next to me.

"Aren't they?" she asks. "I ate one about an hour ago. I was up early and didn't want to wake you guys up. I'm waiting on news from the record label about my client that performed last night. I wanted to be up and fresh if I have to negotiate."

Today, "up and fresh" for her means black leggings and a black sweater with her blonde hair in a ponytail, all of which she makes look stunning.

"How do you feel about his chances?" Dash asks, sipping his coffee.

"I have no idea," she replies, sounding exasperated. "These record execs are as hard to read as the men I date, but he's talented. He got that 'thing' that grabs people."

"He does," I say. "I really do believe he does."

"If only you worked for the record label," she replies. "Tell me more about the break-in. I just can't imagine how terrifying it must have been."

I sigh. "Yeah, well, I was downstairs when I heard the intruder and ended up huddling in the wine cellar in the dark. Where," I add, "I had limited phone service. I called Dash and was disconnected but thankfully he was already on his way back from the store." The partial lie sits uncomfortably on my tongue and I rush past it. "I tried to convince myself my intruder was just the other Allison returning for something she was missing, and she didn't know I'd moved in. But why run when Dash came back? Why run from the police?" I snort. "Maybe she just didn't want to see Tyler. It is his house, after all."

Bella sets her cup down with a thud. "Wait what? You're living in Tyler's house? And so was she?" She blinks and gives Dash an incredulous look. "And you're okay with this?"

"It's a perk of the job. I'm a tenant." I open my mouth to say more, to explain that it's a non-issue now as I resigned from my job, and quickly stop myself. I have no idea how I explain my actions, and no plan to cover Dash in that story comes to me. "And it was a perk of Allison's job as well," I say instead. "Tyler's grandmother lived there. He uses it for the wine cellar and apparently can't insure it if it's not occupied. Bottom line, it got me out of my mother's place without the expense of my apartment in New York and something here."

Bella's lips press together and she just looks at Dash.

My defenses bristle. "I'm not sleeping with Tyler, Bella. I have never slept with Tyler. I'm not thinking about Tyler. I'm not even sure I like Tyler. And neither was Allison seeing Tyler when she left."

Bella's attention whips to me. "I thought she *was* seeing Tyler?"

"No," I say. "Not Tyler. Or not *only* Tyler. I don't know the details, but I get the impression she and Tyler broke up."

"Show her the necklace," Dash says, rotating to face me. "Under the circumstance, I'd say that's a good idea."

In other words, since she thinks I'm playing two men at once, an idea that twists me in knots.

"What necklace?" Bella asks, a nice way of urging me to do as Dash suggests.

I'm not against the idea, and in fact, welcome feedback on what to do about the darn thing. With this in mind, I slide off the barstool and walk to the living room where I've left my purse, and the necklace inside, at some point.

Once it's in hand, I rejoin Dash and Bella, sliding the velvet box in front of her. With a curious look on her beautiful face, she flips open the lid and gasps. "Oh my. This is beautiful. And expensive." Her eyes find mine. "Did Dash give you this?" She glances in his direction. "Did you give this to Allie? And if so, why is she still in his house?"

He bypasses the topic of where I should be living. "The necklace was the vehicle that brought Allison into our lives."

Bella shuts the lid. "What does that even mean? You gave a necklace to a stranger?"

"I decided to stay in Nashville through the holidays to be with my mother," I explain, "but a little extra money to protect my savings felt smart. Thus why I took a job at the Frist Art Museum a few miles from Hawk Legal. That's where I was working when a delivery came for me. It was addressed to Allison W."

Her eyes go wide. "And it was the necklace?" She taps the box. "This necklace?"

"Yes," I confirm. "With a note that read: *Forgive me.* Nothing more. No signature. No return address. I figured out the address was wrong and I went to Hawk Legal looking for Allison. But I didn't want to tell them about the necklace. It felt personal. Especially with the note taken into consideration."

"You should ask Tyler about it," she says. "He had to have sent it."

"Tyler wouldn't send it to the office when he knew she didn't work there," Dash interjects.

"And Tyler knows about it anyway," I add. "I went to that meet and greet thing with him and his father, and it fell out of my purse. I had it with me to go put it in a lockbox and never got the chance. After the meeting, when I talked to Tyler about it, he seemed pretty broken up about the idea of another man in her life."

"Well, any idea that she ran off with the other man is null and void if he sent her the necklace."

My brows furrow with a thought. "Right, but maybe he knows it got lost. I should call the delivery company and see if a claim was filed."

"While that's a good idea," she agrees, "something about this situation feels weird to me. I mean, Allison left abruptly when she was very up and coming at the firm. Why? And of course, logically she *did r*esign and

40

pack her things and leave, or so I assume. If true, that should rule out something far more nefarious."

"She did resign," I agree. "That's the only reason I've restrained myself from going down a rabbit hole of too much worry."

"Barely," Dash comments, rotating to face me, his hand on my knee. "We both know you're barely restraining yourself."

"Okay barely," I admit. "Bella is right. Something feels off about this. You know it does, Dash. And why won't she return anyone's calls? Not even Tyler's."

"Assuming the man who sent the necklace to her was the man she was dating, he clearly didn't leave with her. Hmmm."

"Hmmm never goes anywhere good," Dash murmurs, sipping his coffee.

She ignores him and continues as if he hasn't spoken. "It kind of seems like she's on the run, doesn't it? Maybe from the guy who sent the necklace or even Tyler, though I really don't think Tyler is the stalker type." Her cellphone rings and she glances down to where it sits on the island. "That's the record exec I've been dealing with." She's already on her feet, answering the call. "Hey, Cooper." She listens a moment. "Yes. Yes. I can meet. I'm dressed for the weekend, but—right. I'll be there as soon as I can." She hangs up. "I think this is good. I hope it's good. I have to run." She grabs her purse. "Did you check Allison's social media? And maybe she has a dating profile?"

"She has none," I say. "I looked. That is, speaking of social media. I didn't think about looking for a dating profile. I'm not even sure how to do that."

"I'll check the hot dating sites," she offers, "and see if I can find her, though I'm certain that will be challenging. As for social media, she has an Instagram.

She just uses a cute nickname to keep her professional name protected. Shelly at the office forwarded me a post she did way back when. I'll look for it when I'm at a stoplight."

My pulse leaps at the promise of a link to the woman I've come to know and yet don't know at all. "What's her nickname?"

"A southern girl and her cat," she says. "She has a Balinese kitty. Beautiful girl, too, like Allison herself."

A kitty cat, I think, feeling yet another bond to the other Allison, despite not sharing my home with a furry child. I've longed to adopt a kitty, but my rental doesn't allow it. Cute kitties aside, Allison having a social media presence is encouraging. Really encouraging actually. I now have a new way to reach out to Allison and to check in on her.

"And I'm sorry," Bella adds, "I have to go." She points at me. "If I find out you're seeing Tyler and Dash—"

"Never," I say. "I have never done anything but argue with Tyler."

"With your clothes on?"

My cheeks heat and there's a pinch of anger in my chest that I push aside for one reason: she's reacting to me out of love for Dash. And as painful as it is now, I do appreciate this about her. I like that she protects Dash and as bad as that might feel to him today, I believe it affects his life in a positive way. "There is nothing between me and Tyler, Bella," I repeat, "and yes, of course, I had my clothes on."

She studies me a moment and then says, "Okay good." She looks at Dash. "You know what to do."

My heart races with the potential meaning behind that statement, but before I can ask her to clarify if that

BECAUSE I CAN

means keeping me or getting rid of me, she rushes to the door and disappears.

LISA RENEE JONES

CHAPTER NINE

You know what you have to do.

At this point, neither me nor Dash are on our barstools. We're both on our feet and facing each other. "What does that mean, Dash? You know what you have to do?"

He catches my hip, and drags me to him, his free hand sliding under my hair, folding possessively along the line of my neck. "It means she wants me to do what I want to do and make you mine, Allie. If you'd even let me. But then she doesn't understand that you'll run before I ever get the chance. And you *should* run, Allie."

He's hit a raw nerve and the impact vibrates through my body.

Running and me are synonymous and a little too obvious. Meanwhile, Dash doesn't run, not even from me after I saw him fighting. Or did he? Does he still want me to live with him? He did, yes, he said so, but half a day has changed everything, and inviting me to stay last night is not inviting me to live with him.

I *want* to live with him. I *want* to be with him. And I didn't want to admit that to myself, let alone him, until now. I owe him the truth after all that happened in the past several hours. He's vulnerable and exposed by way of what I've learned, and witnessed, about him, aware of the questions I will surely ask. If I want him to open up to me, I have to shove aside the past. "What if I don't run, Dash?"

"That's the problem," he says softly. "I don't want you to run."

That's the problem.

I'm a problem.

45

And yet, on some level, I understand this and welcome the confession that tells me he might want to walk away from me and us, but like me, despite all reason, he cannot. My hands go to his waist. "If I didn't run already, do you really think I scare that easily?"

"There is so much you don't understand, Allie."

"Make me," I challenge, eager to see behind the curtains.

"That's what you don't seem to get. I don't *want* you to understand."

His mouth closes down on mine, his tongue sliding deep. I moan with the rush of sensation through my body, with the taste of hot man and torment, and deep, biting self-hate. And I'm not oblivious to the fact that he intends for me to find these things, he wants me to feel what he feels, and it's the most honest thing I've ever known. With all his secrets, somehow Dash *is* the most real man I've ever known, and I am suddenly hungry for him in every possible way.

I kick off my shoes, letting him know that I plan to be naked, the sooner, the better. Even as I do, my fingers slide under the tail of his shirt, my palms pressing to his hard body. He tears his mouth from mine, breathes with me, a second dragging into two and then three.

"Dash," I whisper, shoving his shirt up, telling him what I want.

He responds by pulling it over his head. I have a moment, maybe two, to appreciate his sculpted torso before he's turning me to face the island, my hands catching the counter, his lips pressed to my ear. "I'm wrong for you, Allie."

"Do I get to decide that?" I pant out, a flashback of last night with me pressed to the door, his hand on my neck, his cock buried inside me, reminding me of how much he needed control, how much he still does.

"Yes," he says, his hand sliding under my sweater and covering my breast. "You do. Because that's the thing about me being the selfish prick you met last night. Now that I found you, cupcake, I can't make myself let you go."

My reaction is a mix of relief and a surge of desire so intense it clenches my sex. His fingers are on my nipple, teasing it, a rough tug following that, parts my lips in a pant. I moan with the ache building in my sex and Dash drags my shirt over my head, tossing it away. That part of him that's all about control is alive and well, and I won't take that from him. I don't want to take it from him. There's something about this man in control that should make me step back, pause, but instead, he arouses me in ways that astonish me. And right now, there's a furious heat about our energy that is downright combustible. The kind of heat that requires I touch him. I attempt to turn around but his hands scoop under my pants and drag them down my legs. Just when I think this will become a game of push and pull, that is not where he leads me.

Dash's arm wraps my waist, and he lifts me just enough to untangle my legs from my leggings. The minute I'm free, I anticipate his hand on my backside or some sort of teasing in a power-play we both know he will win. Instead, he goes down on one knee, turns me around, gripping my hips, and the look on his handsome face, the combination of possession and tenderness, weakens my knees. Anticipation burns between us and when he leans forward and presses his lips to my belly, I tremble beneath the touch.

Dash squeezes my backside and then one hand catches my leg and lifts it to his shoulder. And there is nothing that feels more vulnerable and yet wonderful, than being this open and exposed to a man like Dash. He knows, too. I see it in those eyes, the window to his soul. He wants me to trust him. He wants me to give myself to him. And after last night, at any moment, he expects me to say no.

CHAPTER TEN

Dash watches me, and I watch him, the burn of our shared desire present and charged, the tug of emotion layering all that is between us, with complicated, and yet somehow, addictive and bittersweet need. Me for him. Him for me. The two of us need each other.

In my life, I've never felt that feeling with any other person. I feel him, inside out and in every way possible.

He leans in and licks my clit, sensations spiraling through my entire body. My lips part and one of my hands finds his shoulder, the other slides into the silky strands of his hair, tangling there. I almost expect him to forbid the touch, to tease me, and build anticipation until it's all but unbearable. I've experienced just how good Dash is at the art of the tease.

As if proving me right, he glances up at me and asks, "Where do you want my tongue, Allie?"

It's then that I realize I've had men try to be dirty with me, but somehow it felt just that—dirty. With Dash, everything is sexy, exciting, and I'm back to the word: addictive.

As for where I want him to lick me, *there,* I think. And there, is everywhere. Okay, maybe I'd start with one particular spot. "You know where," I breathe out.

"Here," he says, stroking a finger over my nub.

I tense with the intensity of my reaction that doesn't allow me to be coy. I just don't have it in me right now, not with his hands on my body and his warm breath promising me his mouth will soon be on *my body.* "God, yes," I whisper.

I'm not sure what he'd expected, but a deep, sexy rumble of laughter escapes his lips and vibrates against my sex, as his mouth closes down, right there, the exact place I wanted him. He suckles me, licks me, his fingers slide inside me. *He owns me*, I think, God how he owns me, and for just a moment, I remember my tears last night, how badly he hurt me. I shove the idea aside, reminding myself that I hurt him, too. And we're here now.

He is merciless in his exploration, licking me, teasing me, his tongue sliding inside me, over me, *all* over me. His fingers slide inside me, stretching me, caressing me, traveling in and out, and all over me. The combination of his fingers and mouth, his tongue, are everything, consuming my senses, and I am so on edge, I can barely stop the tumble over the edge, and yet, I want to, I want this to last.

The room fades, my pulse racing, and I am lost in the moment, goosebumps lifting on my skin, with sensation after sensation, quaking my body. My belly clenches and rapidly radiates downward. I'm panting, moaning, too, I think, though I have no real reality outside of the pleasure, so much pleasure. Dash suckles my clit and I grab the back of the barstool, because oh God, oh yes, he's right where I need him, and I silently plead for him not to move. His fingers pump into me and I arch my hips, lifting, and pumping into his hand, whimpering as that clench in my belly rapidly travels lower and lower. I quake into orgasm, spasms of pleasure, rolling through me. Dash licks me, a sultry sensation that eases me up and then down, with my release, and when he lowers my leg, my knees all but buckle.

Dash is there instantly, catching my waist, and pushing to his feet, his fingers tangling in my hair, his mouth, his mouth that tastes *like me*, slanting over mine. I moan with how badly I need him inside me, and slide my arms around him, my breasts pressing to his chest. Wildness ignites between us and we are all over each other. I reach for his pants. He shoves them down, and kicks them aside, the thick jut of his cock between us as he lifts my leg again, and presses inside me.

I gasp with the shock and pleasure of finally having him inside me, God, yes, finally, he feels so good. Dash lifts me, holding my weight, and easing me backward. I catch my hands on the island, my breasts thrust in the air, his gaze hot, raking over my body, as he trusts, and thrusts, again. Over and over, he pumps into me, his hand sliding between my shoulder blades, and he leans over me, kisses me, thrusts some again.

Incredibly it seems, because I never, ever orgasmed with Brandon, and I mean ever, I'm there again, my sex spasming with an intensity that steals my breath. Dash drives into me again, his hand on my breast, as he groans with pleasure, his body quaking.

"Holy fuck, woman, you're trying to kill me," he says, long moments later, his lips at my ear.

"I'm the one half on you and half on the kitchen island. I can feel him smile, as crazy as that sounds, and he turns me, and sets me on the barstool, grabbing me a napkin and pulling out of me, pressing it to me.

"You okay?"

I laugh. "Just okay? Is that all the credit you give us?"

His expression softens and he brushes hair behind my ear, his touch tender, sending a shiver down my spine. That's how responsive I am to this man. I've just succumbed to not one, but two orgasms, and he can still make me shiver. "You're good for me, Allie."

I catch his hand. "But you don't think you're good for me." It's not a question. I don't have to ask. I know his answer.

It's at that moment, his phone rings where we've each automatically left them sitting on the kitchen island. Dash's lips press. "That thing has terrible timing."

"Maybe it's Bella with good news. You better take it."

He reaches for it and glances at the screen. "It's Bella." He answers the call.

I slide off the stool, and around him, to find a trashcan, and Dash hasn't said much. It's all Bella with this conversation it seems. I start getting dressed and finish pulling on my clothes when Dash ends the call and reaches for his pants.

"Well?"

"No news yet," he says. "She sent us both the link to Allison's Instagram."

"And?" I ask eagerly. "What aren't you saying?"

He folds his arms across his chest, his expression troubled. "She hasn't posted in about six weeks. Up to that point, she posted daily."

CHAPTER ELEVEN

Allison won't return calls. She won't return text messages. She left her dream job and from all accounts unexpectedly and abruptly. "Dash," I say, scooping up my clothes, "This feels off. Don't you think?"

"You have to remember that she chose to leave her job and her home. She resigned, she packed up her house—"

"Unless she didn't," I argue. "What if she didn't pack up her house, Dash? What if someone just wanted her to seem as if she packed up on her own?"

"Didn't she resign?"

"That's what I'm told, but I want confirmation. What if it wasn't official? What if it was just an email or voicemail to Tyler?"

"Baby, I'm former FBI. You know I know how these things work. Right now, we don't have much to stir urgency in the police. She left by choice and until we know more, that's a documented fact. Until that changes—"

"If Tyler tells us differently? Will that help?"

His lips press together with the mention of Tyler. "We just need to know more."

"Can you check in with Jack on her new contact information?"

"He sent me a text this morning. No new contact information available."

"Should there be?" I ask.

"Not necessarily. For all we know, she's local and living with that guy she was seeing and everything is in his name."

Or she's dead, I think, and it's such a horrible thought, I don't say it out loud. "What if she was running away from something or rather someone, and they caught up with her? She isn't posting. She won't reply to messages. I know I'm on repeat, but I'm making my case, to an FBI agent, who I know knows more than I do. Make me feel better about this. Please."

"All of what you said could all be by design," he argues. "Maybe she doesn't want to be found. I've seen that more often than you might think."

One of those raw nerves of mine rears its ugly head and drives my response. "Maybe she needs help, Dash. I mean, if my mom is gone, I'm alone. Maybe she's alone."

He catches my hand and pulls me to him, stroking my hair. "I know how afraid you are of losing your mother. I know how alone just thinking about it makes you feel, but you are not going to lose your mother. And you are not alone. You have her. You have me."

I have him. Do I? I don't really know. And yet, after all that has happened, we're together, we're surviving. Which is why I remind myself to dare to be vulnerable with him, because he has to feel vulnerable with me after all I saw last night, and he *is still* standing here. "I need to tell you why I pushed back at the idea of moving in with you, Dash."

His hands fall away from my body, a clear physical and emotional withdrawal "And why you're going to say no now?"

My heart leaps with the inference that he still wants me to live with him, to call this magnificent apartment, that is only truly magnificent because he lives here, home. "I'm not going to say no, Dash. I was scared. I *am* scared. *You* scare me, and that has nothing to do with anything I saw last night. I have a past, too. I have my own inner struggles. I'm afraid of how badly it's going to hurt to leave in January, after months of waking up next to you, but I don't want to miss that time with you, either. But I don't want you to tell me I'm not alone. I don't want to pretend. We have an expiration date. We have—"

His expression softens, his hands framing my waist again. "Why the hell do we have an expiration date, Allie?" His tone is low, roughened up with emotion.

"My job," I say. "New York. I live in New York."

"Don't overthink this. Don't overthink us."

"I'm not sure how to do that. Not with you." My fingers curl on his chest. "What are we doing Dash? You're not a long-term guy. You said that. You made sure I knew. And I was just fine with that. I was. I really, really was."

"And now?" he challenges softly.

"And now, you already know the answer. I didn't want to live with you because leaving would hurt even more. I'm attached. I'm too attached. You can hurt me, Dash, in a way I didn't even know I could be hurt. I didn't expect that. I'm not prepared for that."

His hand slides to my lower back and he molds me closer. "That's not how this ends, baby. And you're not leaving me. You're going upstairs to take a hot shower with me." He kisses my hand, his eyes meeting mine. "And who knows what will happen when we get there." His lips curve, mischief lighting his eyes, and then to my shock, he scoops me up and starts walking.

I laugh, "What are you doing, Dash?"

"What Ghost would do. What he wants to do."

I laugh all over again. "What Ghost would do? The assassin? Oh God. Are you going to kill me?"

We're already in the bathroom and he sets me down in front of him and cups my face. "It's you who is going to be the death of me, Allie. Haven't you figured that out yet?" He doesn't give me time to argue. His mouth comes down on mine in a searing kiss and allows me to do just what I want to do. Forget all the bad. And focus on the here and now, with Dash. That's the good.

CHAPTER TWELVE

Dash's mouth is still on my mouth when he reaches for the hem of my sweater.

I catch his hand just before my breasts are exposed, and I'm pretty sure that's when we hit the point of no return. "Wait," I say, despite the fact that allowing him to drag me in the shower and fuck me senseless, has its good side, it also has a bad side. We're avoiding an uneasy conversation and the water can't wash away the dirty of last night, anymore than it can erase the unspoken words that once spoken cannot be taken back. And that's what we're both afraid of: the words that can't be taken back. And yet they have to be said. Silence might be gentler, but in this case, it's not better. It all hangs between us, swinging like a blade on a string ready to cut us.

"We need to get the elephant out of the room, Dash. You are stealing yourself from my questions, avoiding them, and me, right now."

"I can assure you, Allie, getting you naked and pulling you into the shower with me, is not me avoiding you."

"It's your way of avoiding the questions from me you expect but that I'm not going to ask."

"Why wouldn't you ask, Allie?"

"I'm worried about you, Dash," I say, his swollen eye driving home that point. "I could barely stand to see you get hit last night but, I won't demand answers you aren't ready, and may never be ready to give me."

His expression flickers with some unreadable, dark emotion, and once again, his hands fall away from me and I can feel his withdrawal that reaches well beyond the physical. I want to grab his hands and put them back on my body, but something in me knows not to push him, not to move, not to speak.

He scrubs a hand through his hair and turns away from me, facing the stone wall encasing the shower just behind it, chin lowering to his chest, one hand on the wall.

I hug myself, not sure what to do, seconds ticking by with the slow groan of a full hour. Just when I think I might have to say something, anything, he rotates to face me.

"I'm a physical person, Allie. I deal with everything I do physically. Before I left the agency, the FBI offered me that physical outlet. Now, I find other ways. I fuck. I lift weights. I plot when I'm running. And yes, I've used fighting as a tool to get out of my own head."

Tyler said as much, but I'm not about to tell him what Tyler said about anything. As I told Tyler. Dash tells me about Dash.

"So it started after you left the FBI?" I ask cautiously.

"The fighting came before the agency. It's how I learned that physicality could be what kept me sane."

"How long before?"

"College. After my brother died, I needed an outlet for all the shit that drudged up in me." He sits down on the edge of the tub. "When I'm running, my thought process is limited. I can't think of anything but the pain of the run and my story. When I'm fighting, it's all about the other fighter and me. There's nothing else."

Only there is. There's pain and I suspect a whole lot of guilt for something I don't understand. But to say that to him would in essence be me diving deeper than I've promised him I will do right now. Instead, I sit down next to him, unable to hold back what I know will be more of a challenge if I'm staring down at him rather than sitting beside him. "And the pain? There's you, the fighter, and the pain, right?"

He glances over at me. "Yes. There's the pain."

I wait, hoping he'll say more, but the more never comes. And while I've promised not to ask difficult questions, not yet at least, there is one I really need to know. "How often, Dash? How often do you need to fight?"

"I haven't fought in years," he says quickly. "It's not a thing, Allie. Not for a long time. You don't have to deal with me and that, as if it's a part of our lives. It's not."

Not for a long time. Not until me. This confession stabs me in the heart and now I'm the one feeling guilty. I push off the tub and step in front of him, cupping his face. "Why last night?"

His hands settle on my hips, his blue eyes meeting mine. "Tyler didn't make me fight. You didn't make me fight, Allie. That was all me."

"Because of me. Because I stir whatever I stir in you that drives you to it, and I drive you to drinking and fighting. Think about it. We're just two messed up people, seeking solace in one another, but finding a new flavor of pain in each other."

"You're wrong," he states simply. "That is not what you do for me. I hope like hell that's not what I do for you."

"Fighting is your drug, Dash," I argue. "It's an addiction and yet, you'd quit until I came into your life." I try to push away from him.

He wraps his arm around my waist and catches me to him, standing as he does, one hand cupping my face, his voice low, raspy, affected. "*You* are my drug, Allie. *You*. I need *you*."

My fingers curl on his chest, springy light brown hair teasing my fingers, and I wish I could just live in the moment, just enjoy what little time I have with Dash, but it's just not that simple for me and him. "I'm not sure if me being your drug is good or bad."

He cups my head and rests his forehead against mine. "Believe me, it's good."

"Then why last night?"

He eases back to look at me. "I was convinced I could fight you out of my system. Just to be clear, I was wrong."

Which he tried to do because of whatever that was that happened between him and Tyler, but Tyler's a bad topic right now, so I leave that alone. Instead, I try to take comfort in the fact most men try to fuck a woman from their system. He didn't turn to another woman, but he didn't turn to me, either. "Because I showed up," I conclude.

His hand slides under my hair and tilts my face to his. "Oh no, cupcake. Don't do that. Don't reduce us to something so simplistic."

"I thought you said not to overthink where this is going?"

"I did and you're still doing it. I was never going to stay away from you, Allie, no matter what kind of beating I took last night. Don't leave again."

"I shouldn't have left," I say, and then stick to my promise to be vulnerable with him, after what I saw last night. "I was running, afraid of getting hurt. It's a problem for me, the running thing. It's something I do to protect myself and I don't like how that looks on me. I'm working on it."

"I would fight a million enemies to protect you, you know that, right?"

My heart swells with the gallant declaration, no one has ever made for me, but I also do so with acceptance. "Some things are not in our control though, right?"

"No, all things are not within our control." There's a hollowness to those words, that echo with an understanding of death.

My hope that we were about to dive into the topic of his brother is doused when his cellphone rings. "That could be Jack. He was digging around for Allison a bit more." He snakes his phone from his pocket, eyes caller ID, and then me. "It's him." He hits the answer button and I give him some space, stepping back, and hugging myself, waiting for news.

The call is short, over before I even hope for good news. "He broke a few rules and had a buddy check her cellphone," he explains, sliding his phone back into his pocket as he adds, "She's returning text messages but calling no one."

My brow furrows. "Isn't that strange?"

"It's a little odd, but she's communicating with other people. That could be a good sign."

Following his "could be" remark, I say what he does not, "Or someone else is communicating as her."

"Maybe," he concedes, "but I don't know enough about Allison to have a solid opinion. We need more to open a missing person's report."

"I know I'm obsessing about this, Dash, but I go back to, what if she has no one to look for her? What if she needs help and we're it?"

His hands come down on my shoulders. "You are not her and she is not you."

"But maybe I ended up with that necklace for a reason? Maybe I'm supposed to help her, Dash. And the only person I know that knows her well enough to put my mind at ease is the one person who seems to be in the middle of everything right now."

"Tyler," he supplies tightly.

"He was emotional over the necklace Allison had received from another man. I think he'll talk to me, but it's going to have to be in person, but I don't want that to be a problem for us."

"You work with him, Allie. I can't stop you from talking to him and I'm not going to try. But you need to know that he would fuck you in a heartbeat, and the fact that you're with me, would be a bonus."

"I don't think he would—"

"I do. I abso-fucking-lutely do."

"I quit my job. Last night I quit my job."

His eyes narrow. "Why, Allie?"

"He took what you didn't want him to take, your privacy, your right to choose what you tell me about you. You'll tell me what you want me to know."

"You're mine," he says, his fingers splaying around my hips. "How is that for what I want you, *and him*, to know?"

His words are pure possessive, and with anyone else, I'd push back, I'd say I belong to no one, but at their core, Dash's words mean so much more. He's telling me, he's all in with me.

"I'm with you Dash," I confirm, because what point is there in playing hard to get with Dash? Or even coy? I'm so tired of games. My life has had far too many and I'm really not a very good player. "And Tyler knows that," I add.

"I told you, he doesn't care. In fact, that's a bonus."

"Why? What happened between you and Tyler, Dash? Why does he want to hurt you?"

He cuts his gaze and my stomach knots before he fixes me in a dark stare. "Because he believes I took Allison from him."

CHAPTER THIRTEEN

Tyler believes Dash took Allison from him.

I don't like where my head goes with this. It feels like secrets and lies are at play, and that is far too familiar. It freaks me out. I try to back away from Dash, but he catches me to him. "You said you barely knew her," I accuse.

"I didn't. I don't. It's not what you're thinking," he promises. "I was *not* dating Allison. I never showed or felt an interest in her. I was at a party and Tyler was there, drinking too much, and showing too much interest in Allison, who was his employee. And he was doing it in front of other employees. She looked like she got the job because she was fucking the boss. Which is none of my business, but Tyler has a history of running through women. I suspect she became one of his fallen, and that means she'd look like a fool at work. And that probably made her leave."

"Is that what happened?"

"I have no idea what happened, but he was neck-deep in a bottle of whiskey that night. I know him, and while most people couldn't tell he was wasted, I knew. She was going to get in the car with him. I called her an Uber. He was embarrassed and lashed out at me. He threw his required professional confidentiality out the door and brought up my fighting in front of her and I was done with him."

"When was this?"

"Six months ago. And as for Tyler confronting me last night. He was being a little bitch, trying to flip the switch, and do to me with you what he perceives I did to him with Allison."

"What does he think you did to him with Allison?"

"They broke up after that. I have no details."

"He behaved badly last night," I say. "But as I think about last night, I don't think he wanted to push you to fight. And I think taking me to see you came from a true place of concern."

"You're right. He threw down and got more than he gambled for. He didn't want me to fight because the repercussions might affect him. He wouldn't want to damage the big paycheck I represent for Hawk Legal."

But that wasn't how it's always been for these two and I'd tell him that I believe Tyler still cares about him, and not the paycheck, but I don't think it's what he wants to hear right now. Dash releases me, grabs my phone from the sink counter, and returns to press it into my palm. "Call him and get your job back."

"I don't understand. I thought you'd be relieved I quit?"

"I got you out of his house. That's what I wanted. You like what you're doing at Hawk Legal and you're good at it. I trust you."

He trusts me.

Words that hit raw nerves.

Trust matters. I want to be trusted and to give trust, but trust has been cruel to me, so very cruel. Dash slides my hair behind my ear, a delicate touch that sends a shiver down my spine. "Maybe one day, you'll trust me, too."

His cellphone rings in his pocket. "That will be Bella with news about her record deal. I'll talk to her. You set-up your meeting with Tyler."

He steps around me and answers his call.

I rotate to watch him exit the bathroom, with the realization that he's giving me privacy to call Tyler. He's giving me trust. But he's also asking for it in return. The thing is, I do trust Dash; in the general sense of the word's meaning. I don't believe he's lying to me or pretending to be anything he's not. I don't believe he says things that are not true. He has secrets though, things he isn't ready to talk about. But then, I'm no different, I remind myself. I still have my own secrets, and I'm holding them close to my chest, tightly guarded. And I'm really not sure I'll ever want to talk about them. Not even with Dash.

Exactly why I shove the past aside and dial Tyler.

CHAPTER FOURTEEN

Tyler doesn't answer my call. He simply doesn't answer. I'm really not sure what to make of that. I walk to the bedroom to find Dash standing at the window, staring out over the city, rain pitter-pattering the windows. I join him, stepping to his side. "He didn't answer. What happened with Bella?"

"The record studio is lowballing her client."

"But they offered? That's great right?"

"She's not ready to be excited yet." He pulls me in front of him, staring out over the city. For a long time, we just stand there, before he says, "Have you ever been to Boston, Allie?"

I rotate to face him, leaning on the steel beam that runs down the window. "I haven't. Do you miss it?"

"Only the memories of my mother. My father still has a place there which is why I just told Bella to turn down a signing there."

"Oh. Don't you want to go back there for you? For your mother?"

"I prefer the memories of her without him. I need to go run, baby. You up for a workout?"

I don't point out his present physical condition because as he said he's a physical person. He deals with whatever is bothering him by moving his body. And so, I say, "Yes. I'd love to workout." Which is true. I've been eating like crap and my arteries have to be clogging up. What I don't do is ask questions. This is what he needs, and it's not fighting. I'm along for the ride, and happily.

We dress for our activity and head to his home gym, okay our home gym as long as I'm living here, and it's pretty impressively equipped. Dash is on the treadmill in about a minute flat. He runs like he's running for his life and I don't even think about asking how much of his frustration has to do with Boston, his father, and the brother he lost. I don't have to. I know it does. I just don't know how it all comes together and drives him to this underground fighting self-punishment. Tyler said as much. This all started when Dash's brother died. Dash lets his opponent beat him up until he's had enough, and he finally fights back.

But the only way this works is if I do, and I can only hope that one day, in the not-so-distant future, I will.

CHAPTER FIFTEEN

Dash and I throw on comfy clothes, sweats, and T-shirts, order tacos, and stuff our faces on the living room floor with the intention of working after our bellies are full. He's more himself now, his mood distinctively lighter. Even his bruised and abused eye looks far less swollen after I forced him to do the whole ice/heat rotation after our workout. And since I keep arnica for bruises and puffy eyes, I've got him slathering that on every few hours, as well.

"I can't believe you got pineapple on your tacos," Dash says, finishing off a chicken taco of his own.

"It's good," I say. "And it's not only pineapple. It's chicken and pineapple. You should try it."

"No way," he says, rejecting all. "No pineapple on my tacos. Never gonna happen."

I laugh and sip my diet Sprite which I was thrilled to find out the restaurant stocked. No one ever does. "Experience threads through books. You can use tacos in your book, but you have to taste them to describe them."

"Well hell, bring on the pineapple then." He motions to my plate. I offer it to him and he dives in for a daringly large bite, then grunts. "I still don't like pineapple on my taco but I'm superstitious enough about my writing that if I have a good day, that's my new taco."

"Well then get to work," I say, swishing a make-believe whip. "Words. Write the words."

"Yes ma'am," he says, offering me a salute.

"I'll make coffee. After the night we had, we need coffee."

"Yes, we do," he says, his eyes lighting with mischief. "You might just make me love you, baby, if you keep all this coffee business up."

My belly flutters with the words, that take me way, way off guard. "I ah—well, wait until you taste the coffee. I'm not the best brewer, but I try hard." With that, I try to stand.

Dash catches my hand, his voice low, roughened up as he says. "I'm glad you're here, Allie."

The comment surprises me, pleases me, takes me off guard, but perhaps it shouldn't. There's a notably new intimacy between us since our little bathroom chat. Almost as if we both sense we're stronger for almost breaking up, and choosing to fight our way back to each other.

"I'm glad I'm here, too."

Spontaneously, I lean over and kiss his cheek. He catches my head and drags me closer, kissing me properly before he says, "Hmm. You taste like Pineapple."

"So do you," I assure him.

"And you," he says. "I taste like you, Allie. And that's a good thing."

I'm smiling when he releases me and I head into the kitchen. Once I have a cinnamon flavored coffee brewing, I text Tyler: *I tried to call you. I'd really like to meet and talk.*

While I wait for a reply and the brewed coffee, I prepare two cups with a sweet cream flavored creamer from the fridge. Tyler hasn't replied but my mother apparently texted me hours ago: *Can you and Dash come for brunch tomorrow?*

My mother is now asking for Dash. Isn't that something? Oh, what an impression he's made on her, and on me. I never took Brandon to meet my mother.

But then, he was close to my father, and my mother wasn't thrilled with my father being back in my life. I found out why the hard way.

But that was the dirty past. This is now. Dash is now. I fill our cups and rejoin him in the living room, noting his complete absorption in his work. Since I don't want Dash to feel I'm looking over his shoulder, nor do I want to break his rhythm, I set my mug and phone at the opposite end of the coffee table. After which, I set his mug next to him and I don't think he even knows which is good. He needs to write that book so the rest of us can read it.

I text my mother a reply of: *He's on deadline. I'm cracking the whip on him. If he makes word count, his reward will be your waffles.*

My mother is not dissuaded: *Tell him he can write over here while I read over his shoulder.*

She and I exchange a few more messages before I settle in at my side of the coffee table and open my MacBook, with the intent of working, but my mind is on Tyler and Allison. Tyler still hasn't replied to my message. It seems as if he's done with me at this point, but that just feels off. He involved me in what happened last night. He had an agenda that involved me. But I did leave him high and dry on the house and the auction, or so he thinks.

I text him again: *I'm not going to drop the ball on the auction. I'm committed to my commitment. Can we meet?*

He replies with: *My office, Monday morning, eight am.*

I reply with: *Can we talk sooner than later?*

His answer is simple and fast: *That is sooner than later.*

I give up. He wants Monday. Monday it is. I set down my phone and sip my coffee. Dash glances at the coffee cup as if it's just arrived, picks it up, and lifts it in my direction. "Thanks, baby."

I smile and lift my cup to him. Dash stares at me a moment, his expression unreadable before he seems to force himself back to his work. If only I could crawl into his head and read his thoughts.

Turning my focus to my MacBook, I intend to key up my work email, but somehow, I end up on my iMessage, finding the text message Bella sent us earlier with the details on Allison's Instagram. I click on the link and Allison's page loads. I'm a bit stunned to discover thirty thousand followers and I'm eager to find out why. I'm also struck by just how pretty Allison is in the photo of her next to her Instagram name, "A southern girl and her cat." Even more so when I scan down to the last photo posted, which is of her and her kitty. With long dark hair, and a complexion of ivory perfection, I decide Allison isn't pretty. She's beautiful. No wonder Tyler was enamored with her, and even broke his rules, about dating someone from the office to be with her.

She's stunning.

And so is her kitty.

I click on the photo of her and her kitty, who is also a pretty girl with white fur and striking blue eyes, to read: *Have you ever had one of those moments when you realize you like most animals more than most of the humans in your life? Humans often disappoint me, especially as of late. Animals never do. Animals don't judge you or desert you. They don't lie to you. They don't ignore you. They will always be there for you, always love you, always be happy to see you. Love an animal today. I promise you, you'll be loved in return. #Balinesecat #animals #bestfriendsareanimals*

BECAUSE I CAN

I stare at the post, reading it again, and I read the familiar heartbreak beneath the words. Someone hurt her. Someone betrayed her. And now, she's gone. I'm not sure what to do with that.

CHAPTER SIXTEEN

I glance up to find Dash focused on his computer, too much so for me to tell him what I've found out about Allison, which really isn't that much at all anyway. I find myself curious about where she was before she was here in Nashville? Or was she always in Nashville? For some reason, I think no. Maybe she's back home, wherever home is for her. What if she has no one to go home to? I think again. If I'd lost my mother, that would be me if something went wrong in New York. I shove away that thought. I'm not going to lose my mother. I'm not. She is over her cancer.

With my stomach in a knot, I grab my phone, and text my mother: *Waffles and brunch, aside. How are you?*

My attention is back on Allison's Instagram feed. I decide to tab back through her past posts and read forward in an effort to get a feel for what changed for Allison between then and now. I find a post from a year ago. Allison is dressed in a sparkly black dress and her post reads: *I've been in Nashville for only six months, but I already know that Nashville nights are exciting, wild, and always filled with something special. Tonight I have a formal work event and I have to tell you I'm feeling spoiled tonight in a dress and shoes by Gucci. I grew up in a humble home with a mother who was a nurse, and a father who was a computer programmer. I saved my money to go to the thrift store, and still go on occasion, there are deals to be found! Both of my parents are gone now, but I wish they could see me now. I'm thankful for new friends, fun nights, and so much more! Oh, and of course, my kitty, Mandy. What do you feel thankful for tonight?*

Her parents are gone and that only makes her question to her readers all the more impactful. What do I feel thankful for?

I eye Dash, and warmth fills me. Everything with Dash feels different than anything I've experienced in the past. Every moment with him is exciting, passionate, fun. When has a man ever been fun to me? And every moment we're together doesn't feel like it has to be entertaining. I'm comfortable to just exist with him. More importantly, I realize, I'm comfortable with myself when I'm with Dash.

I glance at Allison's post again and silently answer her question about what makes me thankful. I'm thankful Dash and I found our way back to each other after last night. I'm thankful for the opportunity to know him, even if it's only for a few months. My phone buzzes with a text and I glance down to read my mother's message: *I'm fabulous honey. How are you? And how is Dash? :)*

I smile and silently add to my prior proclamation: I'm thankful my mom is alive and well.

I must have said it out loud because Dash looks up. "Me, too, baby. Me, too."

Never in my life, have I had anyone to share my fears and joys with, and my heart squeezes with the realization that right now, I do. "I didn't mean to say it out loud. You were on a roll. I didn't want to break that."

He stretches. "I actually banged out a fast chapter." He sips his coffee. "But I'm going back in. You okay?"

"Yes. My mom just texted me and asked about you. I think she's obsessed with the idea of us."

"Good." He winks. "So am I." His attention returns to his MacBook, and mine returns to a photo of Allison

76

in workout gear, holding her kitty that reads: *Mandy is a slave driver. I ran three miles today because she told me I was being lazy. I reminded her she sleeps all day. She snubbed her nose in the air. My reward for my run: I get to rub her head.*

I smile at the silliness and decide two things: I like Allison and I want a cat. I wonder how Dash feels about cats?

The next post is of a man's suit-clad arm, his strong hand holding a whiskey glass. He's wearing a Rolex, and a titanium pinky ring that feels familiar but I can't say why. I don't remember Tyler wearing one. Maybe it's the "other" man? The post reads: *Seduce me, drive me wild. Make me feel like I'm beautiful. A powerful, confident man has always been sexy to me, a seduction in his very existence. But when we're too wrapped up in someone else's power, we can't find our own. I've learned I need my own. I'm taking my own. Own your power. I am mine. Don't let someone else own it or you.*

The post hits home all over again, and in a big way. It's almost as if Allison is talking to me and I wonder how many of her followers feel the same? In my case, I know why I connect with her words. It's really kind of right there in my face. I allowed a man to own me and I don't even remember how I let it happen. I'd thought it was about the wealthy, powerful man I'd chosen to entangle myself with, but I'd been wrong. Dash is far more wealthy, famous, successful, and yes, powerful. It's not about what someone has, but the character of that person.

Lesson learned.

Don't judge all by one. Well, two. My ex and my father.

I shove aside my personal baggage. It's not me I'm worried about now. It's Allison and I'm trying to process what her posts have told me. She's not from Nashville. She was burned and hints at feeling powerless, but now she's owning her power. Is that why she left? Or is that why someone made her disappear?

CHAPTER SEVENTEEN

Hungry for more information about Allison, I begin scanning her Instagram again, and my attention lands on an entry dated September first, almost two months ago. The post is another beautiful photo of Allison and her kitty, but what I'm hungry for are her words, and the look they give me into her life. I start reading, moving from one post to the next, always eager for what I'll discover. One particular entry catches my attention, the photo includes a man in a suit with his head cut off, almost as if Allison is intentionally hiding his identity, which of course, she is. Her words to accompany it read: *"I've never" is how I start every sentence that involves him. I've never known a man quite as striking as he. I've never known a man who walks into the room and my heart races, butterflies fluttering in my belly. Without him, I am lost. With him, I am found. And yet, he stands alone.*

I read the passage over and over again, coming to the conclusion that Allison and I differ, at least for now, in one way. She was in love with a man who rejected her. And I fear that I am falling in love, with a man who is pulling me close now, but will soon do the same to me. I stare at the photo, trying to see the man in the photo as the man I believe him to be: Tyler. It's impossible to know though, but everything inside me screams his name. I saw the pain in his expression over the necklace gifted by another man. I saw sadness. I saw regret.

And yet, she's not with that other man either. Unless Tyler and this other man, the one who gifted the necklace, are not the only two men in her life.

Dash is suddenly with me, settling on the floor beside me, the earthy male scent of him drawing me in, much like the man in the suit did Allison.

"Hey," he says softly. "You're absorbed in your work I see." His gaze lands on my computer screen and shifts sharply back to me. "You're obsessed with her."

"I just feel connected to her, Dash. We share a name. We share the same job. We've lived in the same house. Plus, she has a cat, and I've been wanting a cat. She was in a bad relationship that took over her life and she lost her parents, which hits home because I'm terrified of losing my mother."

"And you know all of this how?"

I indicate my MacBook screen. "Her Instagram."

"You've been reading her Instagram for the past two hours?"

Two hours? I think, frowning. Have I? I glance at the clock, stunned to realize that apparently, it has been two hours. "I guess I have," I say. "I suppose my resignation and inability to talk to Tyler and work things out, has me a bit confused on what to do with the auction. Tyler did agree to a meeting, but not until Monday morning, no sooner. I tried. It was all done by text message. He won't take my calls."

Dash studies me, just studies me, seconds ticking by, and just when I can't take it anymore, he says. "People obsessed with other people's lives, aren't happy with their own."

"It's not about being unhappy." I cover his hands with mine and close my fingers around him, holding on. "It's about the role she played, to bring me right here, to you. She made my life better, Dash. And after last night's break-in, I can't help but have her on my mind."

There's a beat before he says, "Tyler and I need to have a little chat anyway, about a lot of things. He may well know where she's at and why she left. That would end your worry for Allison."

He pushes off the ground and sits on the couch, removing his phone from his pocket, but before he can punch in Tyler's number I warn, "He won't answer." I try to get up only to fall back down. Dash offers me his hand and helps me up and I sit next to him. "He wouldn't take my calls but when I texted him a promise that I won't desert the charity, he changed his tone. I think."

"You think?"

I grab my phone and tab to the messages and then offer Dash my phone. "It's easier if you read it yourself."

Dash accepts my phone, glances at the exchange, his lips pressing together as he does, his disapproval evident before he hands it back to me. "As I said, he and I need to have a little chat, sooner than later."

"What does that mean?"

"It means he's playing one of his typical head games."

I don't know what that means, but I don't doubt he's accurate. This is Tyler we're talking about.

He tabs through his phonebook and hits Tyler's number, but of course, Tyler won't answer. Only he does. And quickly. "Tyler," Dash says dryly. "I think we both know we need to talk."

Tyler replies with something, and Dash says. "Hmm yes. I'm sure my best interest is exactly what you have in mind. I'll see you there." He disconnects. "I'm going to see him."

I settle back on my knees in front of him, and my hands settle on his legs. "Because of me?"

"Because of him, but I will I make my position on you clear, yes."

"Which is what?"

"I won't have him use you to get to me. You're off-limits."

"I can handle myself, you know that, right?"

His hands cover my hands. "You also shouldn't have to navigate the shit show between me and him. That's wrong. Besides, my working relationship with Tyler is becoming too fucking much to manage." He stands and takes me with him again. "When I get back, how about dinner and a movie here at the apartment? Chinese maybe?"

"That sounds perfect," I say. "Yes. Please. Are you going to fire Tyler?"

"I already fired Tyler. The next step is to leave Hawk Legal and that means I fire my sister. And her commission is the only way I can give her my money. She won't take it otherwise. The problem is that Tyler's smart enough to figure that out. He believes I'm stuck with him, which gives him the license to pull last night's stunt. He forgets how resourceful I am. Where's the necklace?"

"My purse, why? Are you going to take it to Tyler?"

"I'm going to show it to Tyler again. You said he blinked when he saw it. Let's see if he'll blink again."

CHAPTER EIGHTEEN

A few minutes later, we're in the closet, sitting on a stool, the necklace box in my hand, as he changes into jeans, a black T-shirt, and black biker-style boots. Dash pulls on a sleek black leather jacket and says, "I'll be back as fast as I can."

I push to my feet and reluctantly offer him the necklace, which somehow feels like letting go of a piece of myself. He slides it into the pocket inside his jacket and folds me close. "Instead of sitting in front of the computer, why don't you look around your new home?"

It's an obvious invitation to be nosey, his way of telling me he has nothing to hide. I've found his secrets already. Only, I'm not sure if that's true. His real secret, or secrets, amount to what really drives him to fight. And I can only hope that one day he'll trust me enough to share that with me. "I'll be sure to dig in your underwear drawer. That's where all secrets are kept."

His lips curve. "Is that right?"

"Of course it's right, though, on second thought, I think I'll just work on the charity event. I'd prefer you tell me your secrets, not Tyler, and not your underwear drawer."

His jaw grits. "My underwear drawer would be more accurate than Tyler. Remember that."

I wrap my arms around him. "Don't let him get to you, Dash."

"He'll be hard hit to get to me today, Allie. I have you here waiting on me, in our home."

My heart softens. "Dash," I whisper.

He kisses me. "See you soon, cupcake. And try to stop obsessing over Allison. Obsess over me."

"That's an easy request to grant."

"Prove it when I get home. I'll lock up as I leave." He winks and releases me, disappearing outside of the closet. I follow him and catch up to watch him exit the front door. I'm alone in his apartment. Okay, our apartment. That's trust. That's an invitation to really be a part of his life. And all of this, after what I saw last night.

Allison left this life behind. She clearly had nothing enticing her into staying. She didn't know the appeal of staying around for Dash Black, but I do.

For this reason, I fully intend to do as I've promised Dash by working on the charity auction, but when I sit down at the kitchen island with a glass of wine, I'm back on Instagram. There's a photo of Allison, holding her cat on her shoulder. Her comments read: *In life, we find good days and we find bad days. We find laughter, but there is also heartache, sorrow, and loss. We feel confident and beautiful and then awkward, confused, insecure, and vulnerable. In my life, I've found only one friend who loves me just as much on my good days as on my bad days. That's my girl, Mandy. If you don't know the unconditional love of an animal, consider finding out. That kind of love can change your life. Four Paws, a charity I volunteer for and love, is having an adoption day on Halloween. Please consider taking home a furry child that day.*

The post touches me, it connects with me and speaks to me, on so many levels. We are all human. We are all insecure and lonely at times. She's just described every reason I want to adopt a cat. And she just gave me my only clue to find her. I quickly google the animal rescue and key the number into my cellphone. After two rings a machine picks up, but the website says they're open. To my surprise, they're located right up the road. I'm already on my feet, headed upstairs to change clothes. It can't hurt to just go to the shelter to see if Allison is there or if they know how to reach her. I do have a necklace to return to her. And I'm not against giving the kitties for adoption a little look-see. I can't get one for me just yet, but my mother has actually been talking about one for a while now.

Either way, nothing can go wrong.

It's just a trip to an animal shelter.

CHAPTER NINETEEN

After changing into jeans and a cozy teal-colored sweater, paired with cowboy boots, I bundle up, pack up my briefcase in case I need it, and head to the shelter. Since it's close, the chilly day makes for a brisk walk, but fortunately not a brutal walk. Soon I discover that the shelter is next to a coffee shop I enjoy, and apparently, I've walked by the shelter and thought it was a pet store many times in the past. Nestled in between rows of offices, stores, and restaurants, it's painted adorably with brightly colored animals playing on the pop of green grass. I open the door and enter a small lobby. A blonde woman I place in her late thirties, maybe forty at most, pops to her feet to greet me. "Hi, I'm Jessie. Can I help you?"

Jessie is wearing a T-shirt with a Great Dane on the front that reads, "Want to play?" The shirt tells me all I need to know about her. She's good people. "Hi Jessie," I say, and despite how silly it sounds I add, "I'm Allie. I'm looking for Allison."

"Aren't we all," she murmurs almost to herself before she says, "And how cute. Allie, looking for Allison. She's not in. Can I help you?"

"Actually," I say, awkward about the lie I'm about to tell, but somehow it comes right out anyway. "I'm her sister from Texas. She's not returning my calls. I'm worried, which is why I hopped on a flight to get here." I hug myself. "She's really alone here."

"Oh my," she says. "I—well—I didn't know she has a sister, and what kind of drugs were your parents on to name you Allie and her Allison?" She snorts but my really bad lie—I'm a horrible liar—doesn't punch back at me and neither does Jessie. Instead, she moves on, her tone turning serious. "I've been worried as well. She's not returning my calls either."

"Did she stop showing up to volunteer? She loves this place. That makes no sense."

"She told me she had a big work project going on and had to take a break, but it's been about a month. I expected her to be back and we're friends. We talk a lot. Have you been by her house? I almost went by myself."

There is a twist in my belly with the implications of what she's revealed. Bottom line, this is not good. "She's not living in the house I knew of anymore," I say. "Someone else is there now. Maybe I have the wrong address?"

"Let's look," she says, motioning for me to follow her. "Come to my office."

I follow her to a doorway just off the lobby where a beat-up wooden desk sits against the wall. She motions to the chair next to the desk and we both sit down. By the time my butt is in the chair, she's keying on an ancient beast of a computer. "Alright," she murmurs. "Let me see. I have an address right here." She reads it out to me, and my heart sinks.

"That's the old address," I say, my brows furrowing. "What is going on?" I give her a pleading stare. "Could this be about that man she was seeing?"

"I think they broke up."

"So is it some sort of stalker and she's running from him?"

"I don't know. She was a little weird the few weeks before her leave, distracted even. One day she came in with puffy eyes. She said it was allergies but I thought it was more like the aftermath of a good cry."

"Do you know his name? She told me she worked with him, but I swear I can't remember his name."

"She called him, 'The King of the World,' never a name. She seemed really in love. I envied her, but then something changed. She stopped talking about him."

"I think she broke up with 'The King of the World.' There was a new man."

"Not that I ever heard about," she says. "The office she used when she was here is down the hall. Last door on the left. You can look around and see if you find anything."

"Thank you," I say. "I'll go by her workplace Monday, but I'm going to go nuts this weekend. Anything I can do to find her is appreciated."

"Will you call me after you see her on Monday? Honestly, I should have tried her office. I don't know why I didn't."

"I'll call you or stop by. It's right up the road."

She squeezes my arm. "Thank you, Allie." She stands. "I'll show you to her office."

I follow her down a hallway and she motions me into a small, private office. I glance at Jessie. "She must be a pretty big part of the shelter to have her own office."

"She has brought in more money than anyone who has ever set foot in this place. She hit up the celebrities at Hawk Legal."

I decide I'd like Allison if I met her. Anyone who loves animals the way she does has to be good people.

"I'll leave you to look around. I have to go back to the kennel and check on the animals. If I don't see you before I leave, is there a number I can call you at?"

"Oh yes," I say quickly. "It's a New York number. I just moved up there. Now I'm kind of wishing I'd moved here," I add, which isn't a lie, not one little bit. I read off my number to her. She punches in the digits. "You should move here. You and Allison should be together.

Life can be fleeting. Family should be close." She doesn't wait for a reply. She disappears out of the office.

Life can be fleeting.

She might as well have punched me in the gut.

Life *is* fleeting, for some more than others.

My mother won't be around long enough, no matter how long she's here, and just the idea of losing her shreds me. But at least I know that, for now, she's safe and well. I don't know that to be true or false when it comes to Allison.

The mystery around her only seems to expand.

CHAPTER TWENTY

I sit down at the desk and pull open a drawer. There's a pen box sitting in the center and I pick it up, flipping open the lid. Inside I find a Tiffany pen, distinctive by the blue color, and worth a few hundred bucks. The older classics are worth thousands, which I know from research I did for Riptide. This one is a thick, masculine pen, which is curious. It seems like an odd thing to leave at the shelter but maybe it's not hers, but a customer's. I don't know. There are a lot of odd things about everything surrounding Allison. I close the lid and seal the pen inside the box, before setting it back inside the drawer. There's a business card next to it and I pick it up, hope stirring as I realize it belongs to a local real estate agent. Maybe, just maybe, Allison left and did so with free will and purpose. Of course, the agent could be someone who adopted, but I choose to hang onto that newly discovered hope. I grab my phone and stick the contact in my address book. There's actually a handwritten number on the back of the card and I input that contact as well, labeling it as "Allison's mystery number." Once I'm done there isn't much more here to see, but I am determined to look harder. I open every drawer, dig around, and do so to no avail. Aside from an expensive pen and a business card that may or may not mean anything, I've got nothing.

Discouraged, I stand up and exit the office. As she'd indicated as likely, Jessie still isn't back upfront. Eager to stay connected with her, I step to the front desk and grab a piece of paper and a pen quickly jotting a thank you note with my number included one more time, just for good measure. I'm just finishing up when the bells on the door chime. A moment later, I hear, "Allison."

The deep male voice is not familiar, but I react instinctively, turning and replying with, "Yes?"

I find a tall, good-looking, dark-haired man, in a custom blue suit and an equally expensive trench coat, standing just inside the doorway.

"You're not Allison."

Unease slides through me and not just because I'm forced to lie again. There is something about this man that sets me on edge. "I'm her sister," I say. "And you are?"

His lips press together, his eyes sharp. "She doesn't have a sister."

Every nerve I own is officially standing on end. This is the man who sent Allison the necklace. I know it with every fiber of my being. "Apparently she does," I say, "and she just didn't tell you. I didn't catch your name."

"Where's Allison?" he repeats.

"She's not here," I reply.

"That's not an answer," he snaps back.

"That's all the answer I'll give a man who won't even tell me his name." He studies me for several heavy beats, and then turns and exits the shelter.

CHAPTER TWENTY-ONE

The man has only been gone mere moments when Jessie reappears in the lobby. "Oh good, I caught you. I forgot to give you my cell number."

I blink and shake myself, not sure what just happened. The man *just left*. It was abrupt and I'm very confused right now. Jessie offers me a card. "This is me. I hope we hear from her soon, honey. I'm worried."

"Me, too," I say. "Has she ever had a man stop by here to see her?"

"Not that I know of, but she's a beautiful girl. She certainly got hit on all the time. Why? Are you worried about a stalker kind of thing? I swear now I'm thinking the same thing."

"No. No, it's not that," I say, *though maybe it should be*, I think, "Not really. I mean, this good-looking man in an expensive suit, dripping arrogance and money, just came in looking for her."

"My God, why can't a good-looking man dripping arrogance and money come in here and ask for me?"

I should introduce her to Tyler, I think, but instead, I say, "It was weird. He refused to give me his name. If he comes back, get his name, will you? And his contact information."

"Of course," she says. "I'm dying to know who he is myself. Maybe he thought you'd know him by name and not in a good way?"

That is a curious thought. Maybe he did.

The door chimes and I'm hopeful the man has returned. Instead, I turn around to find a woman and a little boy standing there. A weird mix of disappointment and relief stabs at me. Almost as if my gut is telling me this man is not a man I want to see again. I glance at Jessie. "I'll call you Monday," I say, waving at her and heading toward the door.

I step outside and a drizzle of light rain is falling, and while the chill in the air is real, it has nothing to do with the tingling sensation on my neck. As if I'm being watched. I scan the area, left, right, across the street, but no one stands out. Maybe I'm paranoid, but I don't like how this feels. I quickly cut left and head down the street, when the rain is officially rain, not a drizzle. One of my favorite coffee shops is a few doors down, and I hurry in through the heavy wooden door, warmth, and coziness, enveloping me. Just being inside the familiar place has me breathing out in relief. I think I'll stay a bit. Maybe I'll have Dash meet me here and walk home with him. Then again, he's a celebrity, and his face is not in any shape to be photographed.

Hurrying to the counter, I order a coffee, before reaching for my wallet. And reach again. My search becomes far more frantic, and the realization hits me. I have my driver's license and one credit card because that's what fits in my smaller purse, which I favor when walking about, or most certainly, for the club. I left my wallet on the nightstand. And of course, this little coffee shop does not take the card I have with me.

My cheeks heat and I quickly apologize to the clerk who thankfully is not familiar enough to know me, before backing away from the counter. I have to retrieve my wallet. That's necessary, and sooner than later. After a moment of consideration, I grab my phone and call an Uber. The car is only five minutes away, but I wait inside until it arrives. The rain is now falling hard and fast, and I run to the car. Once I'm inside I begin a text to Dash: *I'm going to my place*—I stop myself with the realization that my place is now *his place*. I delete the message.

BECAUSE I CAN

Telling Dash I'm going to Tyler's house while he's having words with Tyler is not a good idea. But I'm also not all that kosher with being at that house alone after last night's break-in.

I lean forward to talk to the Uber driver. "Can I pay you to wait for me at the house and take me someplace after? I just need to grab my wallet at the first stop. I left it there."

The woman is mid-fifties, red-headed and friendly as can be. "Of course, honey. You just tell me what to do."

She chats with me for the short drive, telling me about her daughter, who like the entire city, aspires to be a country singer. When we arrive at the house, I hurry to the front door, key in the security code, and enter the house. A chill runs down my spine and while part of that is the fact that the heat is turned low, last night's break-in is clearly weighing on my mind. Eager to just get in and out of here, I hurry through the house, scanning for trouble that surely is not here, before I enter the bedroom. Sitting on the edge of the bed that is still unmade from the time I was here, I realize that I really should have cleaned up a bit before I left. Or I need to clean up. Last night, wasn't exactly the time for such things.

For now, I have a driver waiting on me, and surely Dash will be home soon. I sit on the edge of the bed and pull out the drawer. My wallet isn't there. I know I left it here, but the back of the drawer is quite low, and it might have fallen behind it. I pull it out and a leather book falls out. Of course, my wallet does not. Where the heck is my wallet?

I grab the notebook and set it on the bed, returning the drawer to its rightful place and then search all around the bed for my wallet. It's not here.

My cellphone rings and I sit back down on the mattress and glance at the caller ID to find Dash's number. I quickly answer. "Hey. Everything okay?"

"It is what it is," he says, dryly. "I'm headed home. You want coffee?"

"Actually, I'm not there. I'm at Tyler's house."

There's a beat of silence. "What the hell is going on, Allie?"

"Oh God, it's not what you think, Dash. I went out for a bit and went into a coffee shop and realized I left my wallet here. I just wanted to get it and be out of here. I have an Uber waiting on me. I wasn't taking any chances of being here alone. And I didn't want to bother you when you were with Tyler. I'm leaving now—"

"Just wait there. I'm coming to get you."

He hangs up. A sure sign he is not happy. Damn it, I shouldn't have come. I pull up the Uber app, text the driver an update, and tip her generously. I set my phone down and my hand lands on the notebook. Frowning, I pick it up and open it. The first page reads:

Nashville.

This is for my mother who believed that the best way to know ourselves is with words, our own words.

I suck in a breath, recognizing the handwriting I've seen through my work. This is Allison's journal, and these are her words.

CHAPTER TWENTY-TWO

I'm holding Allison's journal. And while I respect anyone's and everyone's right to privacy, it feels like more of her words could answer so many questions, maybe they even tell me that she is safe. Justifying my temptation to read onward, I flip the page to find a mere one paragraph of writing that starts with: *My first day in Nashville.*

Why am I here, in a city, I've never known before now?

Well, for starters, Nashville is far from Houston, where I'm from.

My God, I think. If this really is Allison's journal, I'm shocked that I got the whole Texas thing right with Jessie. There is so much about me and her that coincides in an almost freakish way, and I can't help it, I begin to read again.

Because I needed to get away, her words read. *I needed a new start. I needed away from everything that once was and no longer is. As for the city, my first impression is that the food is amazing. The energy of the city is amazing. Country music is everywhere. I need a pair of boots. I need a hat. I need a place to live. The Airbnb I'm staying in is small and simple, and no place I can call home. It's a good neighborhood though. I might try to stay around here.*

My brow furrows with her reference to an Airbnb. Is this Allison's journal? Am I wrong about the familiar writing? I glance at the cover and the pages, and it looks fairly new. And certainly, Airbnbs haven't been around for long either, so this writing can't be overly dated. It must be hers, but then again, I don't know how long she was even in this house. Maybe there was another tenant before her. Maybe more than one.

My gaze returns to the text and I continue reading:

That's all. I have nothing else to say. I think I'm bad at this. Writing down my thoughts feels strange and unnatural, but somehow, it's as if I'm writing to my mother. I like that feeling. I miss her. I miss you, Mom. Nothing has been the same since you left.

My heart squeezes with the pain and loneliness radiating off the page. Allison, or whoever wrote this, loved and lost their mother. I can't lose my mom, I can barely even think about it. I can't think about it. I flip the page and read:

Him.

Tall and good-looking, he personifies my definition of the perfect man, all masculinity, confidence, and power, in one hot package. The moment I saw him, my heart beat faster. We were in the elevator of all places, just me and him. We faced each other, stared at each other, and never said a word. Who does that, right? Just stand there and stare at each other? There was a pulse between us though, this tick of sexual tension as if we could come together and start ravishing each other with kisses any moment. And then the doors opened and a crush of people entered the car. I couldn't see him anymore and when everyone cleared out another stop later, he was gone. That might seem like the end of the story, but it's not. I saw him again. But that's a story for another day.

She met "him" in an elevator, the way I first met Dash. And like her, Allison, I am still certain, I couldn't stop thinking about *him*. There's a wave of awareness that washes over me and I look up, and as if I've willed him to my side, Dash is standing in the doorway. God, he's good-looking. Tall, gorgeous, broad, talented, and human in ways too few people allow themselves to be. I shut the notebook, set it aside, and with no hesitation at all, I'm in front of Dash, wrapping my arms around him.

"Hi," I say softly.

He doesn't touch me.

He's stiff, unyielding, displeased, I decide, and for the first time ever with Dash, I have second thoughts about my boldness. I start to pull away.

He catches me to him. "What's going on, Allie?"

I know then that he's read into me being here, seen something in my actions that doesn't exist. "I don't want to be here, Dash. I wanted to just get this over with so I could be done with this place."

"You sure about that?"

There is a hint of what I can only dare call insecurity behind that question, that blows me away. How can Dash Black be insecure? And yet, he is. He so is and I don't know why. Maybe it's the fight last night, or it's something Tyler said to him. Maybe it's just me in this house, but the why really doesn't matter. What he feels, does. "That part where I admitted to falling way too hard for you, you do remember that, right?"

His fingers tangle in my hair and he drags my mouth to his. "I thought you were running, Allie."

"Because I'm good at it?"

"Because it's the right thing to do."

"But you don't want me to?"

"No. No, I do not want you to run. I also don't want you here without me."

His mouth crashes down on mine, the taste of him pure possession. His hands are all over my body. Mine are all over his. Before I can even process what's happening, I'm naked and he is not. I'm pressed to the door, my leg at his hip, his thick erection driving inside me.

It's wild and hot, and there is nothing but the hunger between us, the pump of his body, the arch of mine. On some level, it feels as if Dash is claiming me right here in Tyler's house, for a reason, as if he feels he'll know. It's a thought that could take me no place good, but I can't go there, not now when Dash is driving into me, over and over. Not when his eyes are on my breasts, devouring my naked body. The collision of our bodies is fast, intense, wildfire sparked by our emotions, I don't even fully understand. When it's over, Dash eases my leg down, strokes my hair back, and tilts my mouth to his. "I don't want you to come here again without me."

I notice the way he phrases this. He tells me what he wants, but he doesn't demand I comply. I'm not sure why this house is such a trigger for him, but it doesn't matter. I give him what he wants because it's also what I want. "I don't want to come here at all. And I won't come without you."

He scoops me up, carries me to the bathroom, setting me down in front of the sink. "I'll get your clothes." He disappears and returns quickly, setting my clothes on the counter.

Dash's cellphone rings. "Jesus," he murmurs, glancing at his phone. "It's Bella. Again. I'm telling her this is the quota for twenty-four hours." He turns away and answers the call.

There's a sense of unease in me again, which has nothing at all to do with him taking a call from his sister, but is most likely a component of the dread I feel at the idea of telling him I went hunting for Allison today. I quickly dress, deciding that clothing makes all things less awkward. I flatten my hair presently standing on end and exit to the bedroom to find Dash sitting on the bed, holding the journal.

He lifts it in the air. "What is this, Allie?"

CHAPTER TWENTY-THREE

Dash holds onto the journal, her journal, Allison's journal, or so I believe, and guilt stabs at me, at my invasion of her privacy I can do nothing but justify with good intentions. "I found it while I was looking for my wallet. It fell behind the nightstand." I move toward him, his unreadable, heavy gaze following me until I sit down next to him. "I went to the animal shelter where she volunteers today."

I don't have to explain who I mean. We both know I'm talking about Allison. "How do you even know where she volunteers, Allie?" he challenges.

"Instagram."

"Of course," he says dryly. "Instagram."

"If we as human beings believe another human being is in trouble, it's an obligation to act. It's basic decency. While I was there, a man came looking for her. He gave me the creeps, Dash. He wouldn't give me his name."

"But you gave him yours?"

"Yes, but—"

Before I know his intent, he's on his feet, pulling me with him. "Damn it, Allie, why are you putting yourself in the line of fire? Why?"

My defenses prickle, while that damn journal is right there, between us, in more ways than one. "Don't raise your voice at me, Dash."

He sets the journal on the nightstand, as if he too feels its presence a little too much. "Don't be stupid and I won't."

My defenses don't prickle this time. They blow up in pure white-hot anger. I try to go around him. He catches my arm and drags me to him. "Now you're running?"

"Stop using that confession about running against me. I don't like it. And there's a difference between running and choosing to walk away, Dash."

His fingers curl on my elbow. "Is that what you're doing? Walking away?"

Emotions pound at me. "From the moment, not from you, but damn it, Dash."

"Now who's cursing at who?"

"You're frustrating me."

"The feeling is mutual, cupcake. Real damn mutual."

My hand is flat on his chest now, but I don't push him away, not yet. "You said you trust me. You say I don't trust you. I think you've got this backward. Don't you get how hard it is for me to trust anyone, Dash? And yet, I trust you enough to not even ask questions about last night."

"No, I don't know how hard it is for you to trust, Allie. I don't know anything about your past. You realize that, right?"

"And I know yours? I know what I saw last night, but we both know the answers you gave me were far from everything. And yet, I'm here. And I trust you."

"I trust you, Allie, or I wouldn't have invited you to share my home. This isn't about trust. This is about your safety."

"Really? Because it feels like you're trying to control me. And fucking me until January when I go back to New York does not make you the boss of my life."

I expect him to do just what Brandon did—smash me down, put me in my place, make sure I know who is king and who is the peasant.

Anger blisters his stare. "Is that what we're doing?" His voice is low, almost brittle. "Fucking until January? Really, Allie? Because if all you want is to be fucked, I don't have to want you in my home or my bed to do that and do it well. If this is where you want to be, then be here."

The words stab me right in the heart and then to my shock, he releases me and scrubs his jaw. "Fuck," he murmurs, and when I think he'll say more, he turns and heads for the door.

The room sways with the impact of my past and present, and I realize I've reacted to Dash as if he were Brandon as if that past was the present. I rush after him and just as he would exit the bedroom, I dart in front of him and press my hands to the hard wall of his chest.

He doesn't respond. He doesn't touch me. He just stares at me, and his eyes are now hollow, the way they were last night when I'd found him at that fight event. The only hope he offers me is the fast, heavy beat of his heart beneath my palm, which tells me he is far from as checked out as his actions and words suggest.

Everything inside me screams for me to protect myself, but for the first time in my life, I'm not sure protecting myself means running. "I'm sorry," I say. "I reacted to you like you were a part of my past, Dash. Not my future. And I'm pretty sure that's because I'm so damn afraid of you being my past."

Still, he doesn't react, at least not immediately. He just keeps staring at me, watching me, seeming to reach inside me and weigh the truth of my words. And just when I think he will reject me, his hand slides under my hair, wraps my neck, and he is dragging me to him. "Protecting you is necessary," he says. "You need to know that's a part of me. You need to know that won't change, Allie, nor will I apologize for it. Not now or ever."

To some this might seem like a simple play on words that breaks down to him needing, even demanding, control over me and us. But the thing is, I've known my share of power-hungry, controlling men. That's not who Dash is, at least not with me. And nothing, and I mean *nothing*, with Dash is simple, and most certainly the torment beneath his raspy confession professes this as truth. There are layers to this man, so many layers, and nothing is as it seems on the surface. Dash is a haunted man, tormented by a past that wasn't any kinder to him than was mine. A past that includes losing people he loved.

I tilt my chin back and find his stare, where that torment lives oh so clearly. He has been hurt and everything he does is a product of that pain. He doesn't just need to protect me, he needs more in return, perhaps more than I should be willing to give, but that doesn't stop me from saying, "As long as you know that I'm going to protect you, too, Dash."

His lips lower near mine, a hot breath from a touch as he says. "You can try, Allie. Take me away, baby. If you can."

His words are all challenge and sexual heat. My nipples pucker and my sex clenches in a most unexpected way, considering the punch of my anger only moments before. But then, there is so much about me with this man, and him with me, that I do not understand. But I want to. God, how I want to, but as sure as Dash pulls me closer, there is a part of him I don't know. A part of him that pushes me away that I may never know. But then, there is that part of me, as well. A part of me that I'm ashamed of. A part of me I don't show him because I never want him to know who I once was, who deep down, I still am.

CHAPTER TWENTY-FOUR

It's time to leave this house, but not without my wallet.

"Didn't you have it last night?" Dash asks.

"It's big. I don't always carry it. I just stick my license and my credit card in the card file at the side of my smaller purse."

"And why do you think it's here?"

"I remember ordering my mother some of the coffee beans she loves, and I don't remember ever putting my wallet back in my purse." I walk to the opposite side of the mattress before pulling back the blanket, with me and Dash searching the perimeter with no luck.

"You don't think it got stolen with the break-in, right?" I ask. "Maybe it was kids and they grabbed whatever they could find and ran."

"The security system was turned off. I don't think it was kids. And if the wallet was in your nightstand, it seems unlikely that's the only thing someone took."

We both just stare at each other and let that set in. Because the question remains: who was here, and what did they want? "Right," I say, trying to shake that off and restarting my search.

Eventually, we end up in the kitchen, the journal inside my purse that is now on my shoulder. "I give up," I say, throwing my hands in the air. "It's just gone."

"Maybe it's at the apartment," he suggests. "And you just think you left it behind."

"Maybe," I concur, but even as I do, I'm not optimistic. "I really hope so. If not, I have to call my bank. At least I have my license." I lean on the island and Dash leans on the counter across from me in front of the sink. "I'd say I'd follow you to the apartment, but I just realized I still don't have a car. Did you get any word on the repairs on my car?"

"The mechanic called me when I was with Tyler. It's not good news. The engine's a goner."

"Wonderful," I say dryly. "Now I have no car."

"We'll share until you decide if you're staying or going."

The air ticks between us, our eyes meeting, that familiar punch between us. "You're not the long-term guy, Dash. Remember?"

"I remember everything I was before you, Allie."

His cellphone rings and he scoops it from his pocket, glancing at me as he says, "My sister, and since she just made me talk her off a ledge over this music deal she's working on, I have to take it. Again." He answers on speaker. "Bella," he greets. "Allie is here with me."

"She better be," she chides. "If you lost her that fast, I'd have to tell you what a loser you are. Which of course, you are not a loser. Unless you lose her." She changes the topic, clearly bursting with her need to announce, "They're signing my client! I'm thrilled for him. He's doing a celebration set at Aldean's place tonight. You two want to come back and cheer him on?"

"Not if you want me to finish this book," Dash says, "but congratulations, little sis. You rock this country town."

"Yes, you do," I chime in. "Congratulations to you and him. How exciting and life-changing for him."

"It's an open door," she says. "You never know if they're going to swim in a fishbowl and end up a floater or end up owning the ocean. But that's not the only reason why I'm calling, big brother. We have another studio calling you through me right now. They, too, want to do a spinoff TV show based on the books and movies. They want you there next week."

I wait for Dash to react, to show excitement, but instead, he grimaces. "My eye is the size of Texas, Bella," he says. "You know that."

"This is where you show excitement," Bella rebuttals. "Then we talk through how to handle the eye."

"Exactly!" I agree wholeheartedly. "Dash, this is amazing! This is exciting."

A muscle in his jaw tics. "She knows how I feel about Hollywood," he grumbles, but when my eyes go wide, he quickly adds, "but thank you, Bella. The love-hate thing I've got going on is all love for you and you know it."

"Yeah, I know," she confirms. "Tell the truth. You're a hero. Someone broke into your girlfriend's house and you got in a fight protecting her."

His rejection is instant. "We're not bringing more attention to Allie when we don't even know who broke into the house or why."

"I don't care, Dash," I quickly interject. "If it protects you—"

"No, Allie," he bites out. "No."

"Fine then," Bella says. "You're a former FBI agent, Dash, who still trains with your old buddies. One of them got you with an elbow, but don't you worry, you got them with a knee. There. Problem solved. I'll book it late in the week so you have time to at least get rid of the swelling and make your travel plans." She doesn't give him time to reply before she shifts gears to me. "Allie, did you look at Allison's Instagram?"

"I did," I confirm. "And it's really weird that she stopped posting."

"I have to agree," she replies. "One of us needs to talk to Tyler about where she is." Her phone beeps. "Damn.

I have to go. Call you Monday with the meeting details, Dash. Bye, Allie." With that, she hangs up.

My brows lift. "What about Tyler, Dash?"

"He doesn't know where she is."

"How can you be sure?"

"He told me."

"He told you," I repeat. "Do you even trust Tyler, Dash?"

"Tyler and I are better friends than enemies when it comes to secrets."

I blink. "I feel like you're talking in code."

"Tyler and I were never what I call true friends. He knew things about me and because I was at the wrong place at the right time, I ended up knowing things about him, too. Bottom line, I could ruin him. He could ruin me. As I said, better friends than enemies when it comes to secrets. He has no reason to lie to me. He wasn't lying about Allison. He doesn't know where she is."

"Did she talk to him before she left? Did she formally resign?"

"She did. And this all comes back to him getting too personal with an employee. They were together and then they weren't. She couldn't handle it. She needed a break. It was sudden and abrupt, but it was her free will. He honestly thought she left to allow that work-personal life separation, but then she ghosted him."

"And everyone else. Is he worried?"

"He says this fits her personality. It's not her first time to up and leave a place and do so without looking back."

It all makes sense. It should be comforting, but it's not. "What about the man that came to the shelter today?"

"Sounds to me like she blew him off and he doesn't like it."

He's right. Of course, he's right. He pushes off the counter and steps in front of me, his hands settling on my hips. "Jack has limited resources. I have a friend who left the FBI. He does private hire work. I'll call him and have him discreetly locate her and give you peace of mind."

"Oh God, yes. Please, Dash. Then I can stop worrying about her."

"Will you? If I do this, will you promise me to stop looking for her yourself?"

"Because you're worried she's in trouble and I'll get in that same trouble?"

"Because someone broke into your house, which was also her house. And t*hat* makes me *uneasy*. And because I'm asking you to let the professional do his job. He's good, Allie. I am *not* if you get hurt. Do you understand?"

His voice is low, raw, affected, and this, in turn, affects *me*. Perhaps more so because there is a hint of something in him right now that is not about me, but the family—his brother and mother, even his father in some ways—that he has lost. I wrap one arm around him, pressing the other hand to his face. "I'm not going anywhere but to our living room where you're going to open your computer and write your book."

"Allie—"

"I'll let him do his job, Dash." I soften my voice. "*Thank you* for doing this."

He studies me a moment, his expression unreadable as he says, "Tyler wants you to come back to work."

"How do you feel about me going back?"

His hand settles low on my back and he folds me close. "I can't protect you from Tyler. That's your job."

In other words, he still believes Tyler wants to sleep with me. It's my job to turn him down. "He wants me because he wants to replace her."

"You said it. Not me. Let's go home."

He releases me and we waste no time leaving Tyler's house behind. On the ride back to the apartment, I call my bank and credit card companies. Once that's done, it's done. And only a half-hour later, we're in the apartment, and Dash locks the necklace in his safe.

"What did Tyler say about the necklace?" I ask.

"Not much," Dash says. "But you're right. He's not happy about it."

"At some point, you'd think someone would come looking for it."

"Neil's going to try to connect the dots between it and the sender."

A few minutes later, we settle down in the living room, with both our MacBooks open. And I don't go to Instagram, nor do I reach for the journal in my purse. Because Dash doesn't seem to understand, that *he's* my obsession.

CHAPTER TWENTY-FIVE

For the rest of the weekend, Dash and I tune out the rest of the world. I settle into the apartment, our apartment, and refuse to think about how temporary that might be. I claim my space in the bathroom, utilize certain drawers that are now mine, and take over a small share of closet space. How small doesn't please Dash.

"You don't have enough clothes."

"I couldn't bring my entire apartment to Nashville," I remind him. "I have another closet in New York City. And when you live in New York City, you learn to mix and match, and use your space wisely."

He grunts his displeasure but doesn't push the topic.

We decide that as much as my mother's waffles appeal, this is a good time for us to settle into us. We make breakfast together, workout together, work side by side, and then take an evening walk together. And we talk. That walk lasts until midnight because we just keep walking and keep talking. When we go to bed that night, I'm thinking about his remarks about not really knowing my past enough to fully understand me, which he'd made back at Tyler's house. Nothing about that statement rings any less true and the idea that he doesn't really know me is starting to burn a bit more than expected.

But the past doesn't matter, I tell myself. No matter how humiliating.

I snuggle under his arm, and on his shoulder, and tell myself it doesn't matter. But a little voice in my head tells me I'm wrong.

LISA RENEE JONES

CHAPTER TWENTY-SIX

Before sunrise on Monday morning, Dash heads to the boxing studio for a weekly workout with an old FBI pal, while I'll be heading into my own battle: my meeting with Tyler. "Keep the car," Dash says, palming me the keys at the door. "I'll jog to the studio."

I blanch and recover with instant rejection. "What? No. I'm not driving your brand-new BMW again. It makes me nervous."

He leans in and kisses me. "Yes," he says, "you are." He winks and with that, he heads down the hallway.

I take a step to follow him and halt. I'm still in only his T-shirt that I'd slept in last night. I sigh and give up. It's a short drive. What can go wrong?

Forty-five minutes later, I'm dressed in my favorite black Chanel skirt, a black blouse, a red belt, and a pair of knee-high boots. I grab my purse to slide my make-up bag in and manage to dump it, just like I did the night I was with Tyler and his father. Jack Hawk had picked up that velvet box, opened the lid, and stared at the necklace.

"It's beautiful. Why don't you wear it instead of carrying it around?"

"It's not mine. It belongs to—a friend. I told her I'd ship it to her and didn't have time to get to it today." The lie does not flow easily, but rather, like a lie—awkward and heavy.

He shuts the lid and hands it back to me. "Too bad. It would look lovely on you, Allison."

I have no idea why that moment interjected itself into my mind right now, but it was strange, almost as if he was flirting with me. But I don't think it was about me. Somehow that was about him and Tyler though I'm not sure how or why.

My gaze goes to the journal that is now on the floor and sitting open to a page. I stare down at it, determined not to read it. But it's there, it's calling me, and I pick it up, the words jumping out at me. *I've never known a man who can be as powerful and confident in a custom suit as he is naked in his own skin. The thing is that all people see is that cold, hard part of him when I have seen beneath the man he allows them to see. I've experienced his touch when it was both punishingly erotic and then when it was a tender caress. I've seen that tenderness in his eyes, as well. I've seen vulnerability in him, too, that no one would believe he's capable of ever experiencing. But oh, he has, he does. Why do they think his wall is so wide and high?*

I see the gentler side of him and with that perspective, one day I woke up and discovered, he owns me—in every possible way. I can't change that though Lord knows I've tried and failed. I knew he'd hurt me. I knew my feelings for him were a problem. In his defense, he warned me. He told me he wasn't the guy you take home to mom.

I draw in a breath at what I can easily compare to the conversation I'd had with Dash that first night with him. And yet, I did take him home to mom. And she loves him. God, what am I doing with Dash? What are we doing? My eyes lower to the journal again.

I knew it would eventually transform from pleasure and mutual obsession to pain and not the good kind, as he would call that of our little games. The kind of pain that comes with heartache. I was right, of course. It's happening. The heartache has arrived. I fell in love and I swear I thought he did, as well. I felt it when I was with him. And yet, today I will face him and know that last night he dominated me, had me every which way he wanted me, and I liked it.

Today, I don't. Today is different. And I'm not sure either of us can handle that.

I shut the journal and do so with a twist in my gut. I don't know where Allison is right now, but I know one thing. I wouldn't blame her if she left Nashville. This city was not kind to her. And if Tyler did love her, why did he let her go?

LISA RENEE JONES

CHAPTER TWENTY-SEVEN

I arrive at Hawk Legal with time to spare and am eager to get my meeting with Tyler behind me.

This is exactly why I exit the elevator and I don't turn right toward the main lobby and my office, nor do I head to the coffee bar for the coffee I crave desperately. Technically, I don't even work here. I resigned. Instead, I turn left and head straight to the doors that lead to Tyler's offices. As usual, it seems, his secretary is not at her desk. Almost as if he runs her off or she hides from him. Whatever the case, her absence just makes this all the easier to work through.

I charge down the hallway, willing my racing heart to calm down. I don't even know why I'm so hyped up. I don't need this job. Okay, then again, if I decide to stay here in Nashville, I'm not living off Dash. I don't know if we will even last and even if we do, I'm not going to make him feel his money matters to me. It doesn't. That means I need a job and this job is a good job, and my duties are duties I feel passionate about. Suddenly, the dynamic of this meeting has changed. I'm not as in control as I once thought myself to be.

Tyler's door is open and I step to the entryway to find him standing to the left of his desk, almost directly in front of me, facing the window.

"Come in, Ms. Wright," he states as if he has eyes in the back of his head. And who knows, maybe he does. He turns to face me, and I'm struck by how good-looking Tyler truly is, perhaps more so now than ever as the words in the journal play in my head: *I've never known a man who can be as powerful and confident in a custom suit as he is naked in his own skin.*

"Shut the door," he commands, and it *is* a command. The man oozes in your face dominance, while Dash might have a dominant streak, he manages it in a far less intrusive fashion.

I shut the door and step more fully into the room. "You used me to get to Dash."

"I used you to save Dash," he counters.

"After you used me to punch back at him over Allison."

He arches a brow. "Is that what he told you?"

"That's what *I'm* telling you."

He steps closer, leaving only a few steps to separate us. He towers over me, his expression unreadable as he says, "You used your job against me. That's unacceptable, Ms. Wright. You are in or out. Decide now."

I wonder if he's trying to intimidate me, and I suspect most people would, in fact, respond accordingly. But I work for the Comptons in a business filled with the rich and famous. Not to mention, my editorial experience forced me to critique some of the most talented authors on planet Earth. My chin lifts and I say, "I will not be used against Dash."

"In or out does not require commentary."

"In," I say. "I made a commitment. I'm passionate about the work I'm doing here."

"And after the event is over?"

"Are you offering me a job?"

"You spoke to me about motivations. I'm simply trying to understand yours."

Being near my mother, I think. *Being with Dash. Being happy.* But I say none of this. I stick with what is relevant to his needs. "Right now," I say, "I'm here to make the auction a success but I'm not going to stay in your house, Tyler. Not after what happened the other

118

night." I hesitate and ask, "Could it have been Allison? Did she come back?"

"Allison wouldn't have run away."

I inwardly flinch at what feels like a jab, as if he's saying that I'm running away, but I'm not. I'm here. I'm standing in front of him. And as for the other Allison, the journal tells a story he is not. "Not even if she thought I was your new woman?" I challenge.

There's a tic in his jaw, a darkening of his eyes. "It wasn't Allison."

"You weren't sure when I talked to you."

"I'm sure now."

"Did you talk to her?" I press.

"No. I did *not* talk to her. Go to work, Ms. Wright." He offers me his back and then he's behind his desk, dismissing me with words and actions.

I'm not as easily dismissed as I once might have been. It seems I've changed, grown even, over the past couple of years.

I follow him, stepping to the opposite side of the desk, but I can't seem to figure out what to say. Growth comes slowly, it seems.

Tyler arches a brow at my silent intrusion while I battle over words and the wisdom of speaking that truth. Because you can doesn't mean you should. That is a lesson I've most certainly learned the hard way. I want to tell him how much she cared about him. I want to tell him to find her and tell her he loves her, too. I know he does. I can feel it when I say her name, almost as if he quakes inside. But I can't do that without telling him about the journal, which doesn't feel right. I settle for, "I've been thinking about getting a cat so I went to the shelter where Allison volunteers."

"You've been thinking about getting a cat? But you're going back to New York?"

"Yes," I say. "I've been thinking about it for a while now." I shift back to what is important. "They haven't heard from her, either. When I was there, a man showed up looking for her. He wouldn't tell me his name."

His expression tightens. "His name is Brad Waters."

"How do you know who I'm talking about?"

"I know who is asking around about Allison."

"Okay. So, Brad Waters. You know him?"

"I know him," he says, but he gives me nothing else.

"What if she left to get away from him, not you?"

That ticking in his jaw is back. "Go to work, Ms. Wright."

My lips press together as I bite back a more detailed probe. "I'm going to work."

"Excellent idea. I wish I'd had it."

I hesitate again but turn and head for the door. Once I'm there he says, "If you resign again, regardless of reason, I'll accept it."

I rotate to face him and when I would push back, he adds, "I can either count on you, through all highs and lows, or I can't count on you at all. That is simply how it is and will be."

There's really no pushback to that statement. His house, his rules. I respect him as my supervisor. It's the personal lines with Dash he crossed that I have a problem with.

I turn to face him and say, "Understood. I want to be here. I'm going to do a good job. And on another note, I can't leave this office without telling you that I don't believe she would ghost you, Tyler. Ever." I turn back to the door but not before I see the jolt of pain in his eyes.

As my hand closes on the knob, he says, "Everything is not what it seems, Ms. Wright. Remember that. It will serve you well."

BECAUSE I CAN

There is a vibration to his voice, emotion he doesn't quite check and I'm reminded of the journal yet again: *The thing is that all people see is that cold, hard part of him when I have seen beneath the man he allows them to see.*

And so have I, I think. *And so have I.*

I don't turn around again.

I leave the office. And I do so with more questions than answers.

LISA RENEE JONES

CHAPTER TWENTY-EIGHT

Once I'm in my office, I settle in and realize just how much I didn't want to say goodbye to this place. I really am passionate about what I'm doing here. I'm helping a charity and therefore, helping people in need. I don't think I realized how much I need that in my life. In a highly familiar, and endearing way, Katie pokes her head in my office with coffee in hand.

"Have I told you I love you?" I ask.

"No," she says. "Nor have you told me you're dating Dash Black." She sits down in front of my desk and offers me a cup. "How did I not know this?"

"How *do* you know this?" I ask, accepting the cup.

"One of the girls saw you two together at Aldean's place."

"Oh yes, well we are, in fact, seeing each other."

"My God," she gushes. "He's so good-looking. And talented. And rich. How did this happen?"

"We met on the elevator and he was helping me a bit with the charity auction. Plus, you don't know this, but I was an editor at the publishing house he started out his career at. We didn't meet then, but it was common ground."

"You live a dream life."

I blink at that. I live a dream life. Her perspective gives me some perspective. I've been allowing a bad time in my life to define my entire life. I've been blessed in so many ways, including my mother not just beating cancer, but her just being my mother. And my stepdad is pretty wonderful, too.

"You're living it with me," I tell her. "We're at Hawk Legal doing great things. This is our life."

Her lips curve. "You're right. Too bad Jason Aldean is married. Maybe he'd walk in the door and marry me."

I laugh. "Your Mr. Right will walk in the door one day. Be picky. Believe me, that's good advice."

Bella appears in my doorway, looking like the blonde bombshell that she is in a navy-blue suit dress. "Walk me to the coffee bar, will you?"

Katie rotates and waves to her. "Morning, Bella."

"Morning, Katie," she says. "Don't worry. I won't keep her long."

I'm struck by how sweet Bella and Dash are to everyone around them. No one would know how successful they are from how they treat others. Katie heads to her office and Bella and I walk toward the café.

"So," she says. "Tell me about you and Dash."

"You know about me and Dash."

"I know everything is different with Dash since you showed up, Allie. And that's a good thing." She squeezes my arm and we step into the café.

"Everything is better with me since Dash too, Bella."

"I'm so glad." She places her order and as soon as we sit down, I say, "I moved in with him."

"I knew you living in Tyler's place was not going to fly with Dash. Good. That thing with Tyler was weird. Really weird."

"There was never anything between me and Tyler," Bella.

"I know," she says. "But Dash needs to know, too." Her name is called from the counter. "Be right back."

She hurries to the counter and I smile. I really do like her. She feels like she could become the sister I never had, which is a crazy thought. I'm not marrying Dash. He's not the marrying kind and neither am I. Bella rejoins me, coffee in hand, and says, "This Allison thing is worrying me. She's on my mind. I think we should talk to Tyler."

"Dash met with him yesterday and I talked with him this morning. He doesn't know where she is. And Dash is hiring one of his old FBI buddies to find her, just to give us all peace of mind. I think I'm driving him crazy with my obsession over her."

"I'm glad he did. I really am. That gives me peace of mind, too." Her phone buzzes with a message. "Speaking of old FBI buddies. One of them just saved Dash's ass." She turns the phone in my direction and shows me a photo of Dash leaving the gym with his black eye in focus. The headline reads: *Talk about keeping it real.* New York Times *bestselling author of the Ghost Assassin series, Dash Black, leaves the boxing studio with a black eye after brawling with a former FBI pal.*

My gaze jerks to Bella's. "Does he know about this?"

"He agreed to let me tip off a reporter. For you," she adds. "You know he didn't want you getting dragged through the press after the break-in. And we needed to control the narrative. Now he looks like he's doing research."

"You're good, Bella."

"I'm just taking care of my brother. And you." She squeezes my hand. "I need to go call him and give a heads up to the studio and publisher. Sorry to run off."

"Go. Work your magic," I urge. "We can talk later."

"Let me know if you hear anything about Allison. Oh, and I do have donations for the auction. I'll email you my list this afternoon."

She heads off and I make my way back to my office, eager to get to work. I've just hung up with a donor when Katie pokes her head in the door. "There's a man here to see you. A very good-looking, but cranky, man."

My brows dip. "Okay. Do you want to bring him back?"

"Can you come and get him? Sorry, but when I say cranky, I mean cranky."

"Okay," I say again, very confused right now. Katie has dealt with superstars on their high horses. For her to rattle over this guy says a lot. "I'll go to the lobby."

"Thank you," she says and backs out of the office.

I walk down the hallway and around the front desk, to enter the lobby. The man is facing the elevators, his phone in his hand. A pinch of familiarity is instantly with me, as is a sense of unease. I walk toward him and halt. He ends his call and turns to face me, and I am staring into a familiar face, fixed in a steely gray stare.

This is the man from the shelter. "Who are you?" he demands.

"Allison."

"You're not Allison," he says tightly, arrogantly even. "And you're not her sister, either."

CHAPTER TWENTY-NINE

The stranger and I stare at each other.

"Who are you?" I ask softly, though of course, I know from Tyler, his name is Brad Waters.

"Who are *you*?" he asks, not so softly.

I play his game, seeing where it will lead. "You don't seem to like to give away your name."

"Brad Waters."

At the sound of Tyler's voice, Brad shifts to place us both in profile.

"Tyler," he greets.

Tyler gives me a flick of his gaze with a command. "Go to your office."

I give a quick incline of my chin and turn and start walking, but before I enter the hallway, I turn back to see the two men standing toe-to-toe. Their voices are low but their spines are stiff. These were the two men in Allison's life. And yet, neither seem to know where she is right now. I don't know what transpires between the two men, but Brad steps around Tyler and walks toward the elevator. Tyler watches him until the moment he steps on the elevator, as do I. As if he senses me there, Tyler rotates and brings me into view, arching that arrogant brow of his, with a silent question that is pretty obvious: why am I still here?

I give him a short nod, and back into the hallway, not sure what to make of anything that just happened. Katie pokes her head out of her door and mouths, "What was that?"

I hold my hands out and silently reply, "No idea."

She meets me at my office door. "Do you know who that man was?"

"Brad—"

"Waters?" she asks incredulously. "As in the money man Brad Waters?"

"Yes. I think so. He was looking for Allison. Why is that a big deal with all the big names we have come through here?"

"He's like Elon Musk but I think he's one of those hedge fund, finance guys. Crazy wealthy. He's richer than most of our biggest stars," she adds. "For him to come here in person just seems weird. Which reminds me, did you ever hear from Allison?"

"Sadly, no. I sure could use her input."

"I don't think she's coming back," she declares. "Otherwise, she'd be more willing to help."

She's right, of course.

Allison isn't coming back.

The question is, why?

CHAPTER THIRTY

While I trust Bella immensely, I can't help but wonder how Dash truly feels about his newsworthy black eye. I shut my door and hurry to my desk with the intent of calling him, but I've barely sat down before I'm being connected to a client you might as well call Hawk Legal royalty, she's so high-profile. Her generosity with her donations turns into a lengthy conversation. I blink and an hour has passed, and yet another call, followed by another, consumes me. Nowhere in the middle of it all, do I have a moment to talk to Dash. It seems one of the agents in the office decided to start his day by challenging all of his clients to call me and donate to the auction. Apparently, I represent good press and a tax deduction. I could be worse things, I decide. I'll take the connection and take it readily if the charity benefits.

Another call comes in, there's a knock on the door, and I'm answering the line while Katie is stepping into my office to ask a question. Chaos continues until *finally* the calls die down a bit and I glance at the clock to find it's nearly noon. I don't know where this day has gone or how Katie would have survived if I wouldn't have come back to work. I reach for my cellphone to call Dash only to have him appear in the doorway. He's in black jeans and a long sleeve, fitted black T-shirt, with a contrasting tan blazer and just the sight of him sets my pulse racing in a way no other man has ever done. "Hey," I say, standing. "How are you?"

"You mean am I pissed at my sister's stunt with the press?" He closes the space between us and rounds my desk, catching my waist, and turning me toward him, heat radiating from his palms, branding me, "Hi there, cupcake," he says all soft and raspy. I really love when he does that soft, raspy tone.

"You and the cupcake thing."

"You know you like it," he teases.

What girl wouldn't want this man to have a silly and somehow sexy nickname for her? I think. "I guess it's kind of our thing now," I say, "and on another note, I hear Bella played fixer-upper with your reputation. Did that all work out okay for you?"

He sits on the edge of the desk. "She kept you out of the spotlight and answered a lot of questions I didn't have to. The Hollywood people are impatient. They can't wait until the end of the week to talk. We're doing a conference call with them. You have time for a fifteen-minute lunch in the café?"

"You do know the entire place is going to talk about us, right?"

"Not if you treat me like a client and keep your hands off me," he says, grinning. "But we both know you can't do that. I don't care what they talk about, baby. We're together. Unless it bothers you, let them talk."

"It doesn't bother me."

Approval lights his eyes. "Then feel free to put your hands all over my body."

I laugh and the truth is, his reaction pleases me. It's also the first time in my life I've ever really felt what I feel right now with Dash. And I can't even explain what that is. It's just right and good and more different than anything I expected to feel or even knew I could feel. "All right then," I say. "Egg salad sounds good and they do have them prepped in the cooler."

"Egg salad it is," he says warmly, his eyes alight with approval of my reaction as if I've just agreed to a coming out of sorts. And I guess I have.

We exit the office and head to our left, toward the café. "You'll be pleased to know that I didn't wreck your car," I inform him.

His lips curve. "That's good to hear. I got you a car to use while you're here. It'll be here tomorrow afternoon."

"You got me a car?" I glance over at him. "As in a rental?"

"Something like that," he says noncommittally, holding the door to the café for me. "You'll see when it gets here."

I'm curious about the car, of course, I am, and that should be what is in my mind, but the "while you're here" comment he made is what really kind of dampens my mood. We're both living like I'm leaving, aren't we? I seem to be going back and forth and all over the place in my assessment of me and him.

"You didn't have to do that," I say, wondering the cost of the car, not wanting him to have to pay my way, and needing to control my spending.

"No," he agrees. "I didn't have to do it. But I wanted to."

His words and his eyes are warm all over again, and while I want to object to him spending money on me, we're already at the café counter. For now, I focus on food. We each make our selections and settle in across from each other at a small, intimate corner table. "Do you think the whole press thing worked?" I ask, opening the plastic container holding my sandwich.

"It's our story and I'm sticking with it," he says, and while he digs into his sandwich, I'm wondering how he dealt with the aftermath of his fighting in the past. Because obviously, this isn't his first rodeo where that's concerned.

The bottom line for me is that Dash enchants the world with his stories but it's *his* story, his real story, that I want to know. I wonder if I will ever truly know him. For now, though, I set aside the hunt for his real self and focus on this day and this moment. "Something weird happened today," I announce.

"Weird how?"

"Remember how I told you that man showed up at the shelter?" I ask.

His lips press together. "The one you gave your name and didn't get his?"

"Yes," I say primly. "That one. That man showed up here today asking for Allison. The staff thought he was asking for me so I met him in the lobby. He was confrontational with me, demanding my reason for being here at all. Tyler showed up just in time and sent me away, but I lingered and watched them interact. They had words, not good ones, and then the man left. Apparently, he's some really wealthy finance guy. Brad Waters is his name."

"Brad Waters," he says. "Interesting."

"Interesting how?"

"Aside from the fact that Hawk Legal represents some of his brands," he says, "he and Tyler have a colorful background."

"How colorful?" I ask.

"Our time right now is way too limited for that topic. I'll leave it at that until later when I'm certain you'll pick my brain." He changes the subject. "I guess you decided to see the auction through at Hawk Legal?"

I hesitate to drop the subject of Brad, but I accept the swift change of topic with his promise of more on the Brad topic later. "Tyler and I talked," I state. "I told him I won't be used against you. He, of course, told me if I resign again, I'm gone for good. Paraphrasing, of course, but that's the general gist."

"Of course," he says, dryly. "That signing I have in New York is a charity event on Halloween weekend. Books for Kids is a good organization that strives to stop illiteracy. You're passionate about books and reading, and so am I. And yes, I'm trying to sell you on why you should go with me. And as a bonus, I can see your apartment."

Any pleasure I have over his invitation is quickly replaced by rejection. "No," I say, images of his glorious home in my head, our home, right now, I correct. "It's tiny and embarrassing."

He leans in closer and softens his voice. "You don't have to be embarrassed about anything with me, Allie. You know that, right?"

"I do know that," I assure him. "You don't make me feel less than you, Dash."

"What do I make you feel, Allie?"

"Too much, Dash," I reply softly. "Too much."

His eyes lower to my mouth, lingering as if he's wishing he could kiss me as if he's thinking about doing it anyway. "Tell me about the guy who burned you, Allie."

My pulse races. This is a topic I do not like, not one little bit. "Right now?"

"Yes. He's in New York?"

"Yes. I thought our time was limited."

"Give me the condensed version."

"I didn't live with him, if that's what you're getting at, but I was sort of, actually, engaged to him."

His brows shoot up. "Engaged. Alright. I didn't expect that. For how long?"

"Three months. The minute I said yes, he changed. Or maybe I changed. I don't know. I never felt for him what I—" I stop myself. God, what was I about to say?

Dash narrows his eyes on me and he catches my hand under the table. "Finish that sentence."

I comply. Almost. Not quite. "I told you how I feel about you, Dash. And it's not how I felt about him."

"And yet you said yes?"

"It's complicated. If we were two pieces of a puzzle, we wouldn't be working on the same puzzle."

"And what are we?"

"Confusing. Undefinable."

"Agreed," he says. "You are nothing if not unexpected, cupcake."

"I don't know what that means."

"Neither do I, but we'll figure it out together." He glances at his watch. "Damn. I have to get to my meeting."

"And I need to give you the car keys."

"Keep them, baby. I'm going to walk to the bookstore to sit there and write anyway. I'll just stay there until you can meet me."

"I should be able to take my work home by late afternoon."

We enter my office and linger in the doorway, as he says, "Halloween is a Sunday but the signing is Saturday. Why don't we leave Wednesday? That gives you time to go to Riptide, check on your apartment, and for me to take you to your favorite restaurant there."

Not his favorite restaurant. Mine. "I'll talk to Tyler and see if I can make it happen."

"Remind Tyler that a charity event is a great place to find people willing to donate."

He leans in and kisses me. "I'll see you soon." He exits the office then, but the scent of him, earthy and male, lingers in the room and teases my nostrils.

I'm still standing there, thinking about that undefinable something that is me and Dash, when my phone buzzes on my desk. Sighing, I sit down and grab the receiver. "Allison Wright," I greet.

"Ms. Wright."

The male voice is familiar, too familiar for my limited contact with the man. It's Brad Waters. Suddenly on edge, I proceed with caution. "What can I do for you, Mr. Waters?"

"We should meet and don't ask why. We both know why."

Unease slides through me. "You can come back here."

"We both know that's not an option. Pick a location. I'll meet you there."

I could say no, but he's a powerful man. He's also a client of Hawk Legal. But that said, having been raised by a protective mother, I play it safe. "Cupcakes and Books in fifteen minutes." And just for safe measure, I add, "My friends own it."

"Fifteen minutes," he confirms and disconnects.

LISA RENEE JONES

CHAPTER THIRTY-ONE

I arrive at the bookstore through the bakery entrance, scanning the seating area to find the odd hour of two o'clock a quiet one, with all seats free. Adrianna is behind the counter, her long hair silky and beautiful around her shoulders, her smile bright as she greets me. "Hello, my love. We haven't seen you in a few days."

"Busy, busy, working on the charity event. Which reminds me, I need to order the cupcakes before you get booked, but now is not a good time. I'll come by tomorrow."

"That works. I haven't seen Dash in here lately either. Did you edit his book?" She wiggles her eyebrows, most likely not talking about editing a book at all.

But I play dumb and reply like she is. "No, I didn't edit his book. And he'll be in soon."

"He will? And you know this how?" Her smile is wide. "Are you two—"

"We are actually," I say. "I guess you were right about how he looks at me."

"And how *you* look at *him*. I need to know everything."

The bells on the door chime and I turn to find Brad entering the bakery. I eye Adrianna. "We'll have to talk later. I have a work meeting."

She in turn eyes Brad Waters, Mr. Money, power, and good looks, in an expensive suit, and then looks at me. "Work?"

"Oh yes," I assure her. "And not a pleasant meeting either. That's why I picked here. You can be my bodyguard. I'll take my normal coffee. No cupcake right now. The last thing I need is to try and eat in front of this man."

"You got it, honey," she says. "I'll bring it over. Good luck."

I turn and bring Brad into full view. He motions toward a table. We both walk in that direction and sit down. I slide out of my coat, settling it on the back of my chair. He's not wearing one of his own. Perhaps the entire idea of taking it on and off feels weak to him. I think it must. On that note, I don't bother to offer him coffee. He's the kind of guy you could insult by assuming he can't handle his own drink requests. His eyes are gray. That's the first thing I think when I meet his stare. A cold gray. Icy. Brutal.

"You look like her," he observes.

I blanch when I shouldn't. I mean it's not the first time the comparison has been made. It's just the flat way he announces his own observation, without so much as a greeting.

"Not really," I say, recovering from his unexpected remark. "I've seen her photos. Our colorings are the same. That's about all."

"And your name."

"I go by Allie."

"But you were born Allison." He doesn't give me time to confirm the obvious. "Are you her sister?"

Obviously, he's now questioning all he thought he knew about Allison. "No. We're not sisters."

I steel myself for him to ask why I lied about such a thing. Instead, he asks simply, "Do you know where she is?"

"No," I say, watching him for a reaction, as I add, "and she seems to have walked away from Hawk Legal in a firm way. She doesn't even return messages."

"My experience as well."

"I know you're a client of Hawk Legal, Mr. Waters," I say.

He folds his hands together in front of me and my gaze goes to his pinky finger, seeking the ring on Allison's Instagram, but it's not there. "I'm sure Tyler told you that and plenty more," he assumes.

My gaze jerks from his hand to his icy gray eyes. "Tyler told me nothing. I'm resourceful on my own."

"Gossip gets around," he says, clearly jabbing at my resourcefulness.

I slide right by that remark. "I hardly call the staff knowing a high-profile client, gossip. Who are you to Allison?"

His eyes darken. "No one she would walk away from."

"Because you're rich and powerful?" I challenge.

"Because I'm an asshole she couldn't possibly want for more than money and power?" he counters.

His expression is unreadable but there is something about the inflection in his voice, the darkening of his eyes that tells a story I cannot quite read. In that moment, I wonder if the man in the journal could be him, not Tyler. Except that in the journal the man left her, not the other way around. Unless, the tide shifted, and she got tired of his games and walked away herself.

"I know nothing about you," I say.

"I'm all over the press."

I think of Dash's fight coverage Bella set up and say, "I have no doubt. But none of that is the real you."

Adrianna sets my coffee down next to me and then eyes Brad. "Can I get you something, sir?"

"Nothing," he says, and to my surprise, he looks at her and says, "Thank you."

It's the first sign I've had that this man is human, and I'm not quite sure how to define him now more than ever.

Adrianna smiles at him and walks away. Brad reaches in his pocket and sets a card in front of me. "If you talk to her, text me. I'll pay you well for the contact."

"I don't want your money. And I don't know if she wants to make contact. But I'll tell her how much you do."

He studies me several beats and then inclines his chin. He starts to rise but hesitates, long enough to meet my stare and say, "You have her eyes," before he's on his feet, striding away.

CHAPTER THIRTY-TWO

I watch Brad Waters exit the coffee shop, with his words in my head: *You have her eyes.*

I'm officially creeped out. I shake off the meeting and when I face forward again, it's to realize that Dash is now standing above me on the opposite side of the table. "Hi," I say, blinking him into view, only to realize that aside from looking like a tall, delicious drink of hotness, he's scowling.

He sits down in front of me. "What the hell was that, Allie?"

"He called and—"

"He called and the guy who creeped you out convinced you to meet him? And you didn't call me?"

"You were in a meeting with Hollywood, Dash, and I knew I'd be safe here. And he's a client of Hawk Legal. I'm doing my job."

"We both know you meeting him was not about your job. What the hell were you thinking, Allie?"

"You're being confrontational, Dash."

"Because I won't sit back and let you get hurt."

"He's just worried about Allison. That's all that was."

"Is he? Because my man looking into her location can't find her. At all, Allie. She's a little too MIA for either of us to feel comfortable. And right now, Brad's reading like a stalker."

"You're worried about her, too, now," I say flatly. It's not a question. It's just me saying out loud what I already know. I'm not crazy. Something is wrong. Something happened to Allison.

"Right now, I'm worried about *you*," he says. "You know you resemble her, right? And before you read into that, I mean, just enough that you fit a type. And I don't like that."

"He said that, too. Brad. He said I look like her."

His expression tightens. "Did he now?"

"Yes, and while that sounds creepy all over again, I know, I don't think he hurt her. He wouldn't be looking for her if he knew where she was."

"Or maybe he would. You have no idea the things I've seen. Don't do something stupid like this again."

"*Stupid?*" I demand, bristling all over again. "Did you really just say that to me, Dash?"

"Your actions, not you, Allie. I'm protecting you. We've had this conversation. I'm going to protect you, Allie. That's non-negotiable."

The bells on the door chime and I draw in a breath, trying to calm myself. I know Dash is worried about me and while that feels good, I'm also sharply and acutely reminded of that need for control he possesses. A need that comes from a dark place of pain and torment, that I can't begin to understand but I believe it has to do with loss and death. Which means caring about me and believing I'm in danger in some way, has triggered him. But him being triggered is triggering me as well. I ran from my past, and part of that past was the control everyone but me had over me, to the point that I didn't even recognize myself. And while I know that's not Dash, I know that's not his intent, right now, I just need a little space.

I need to breathe.

"I'm going to freshen up," I say, grabbing my purse.

I don't wait for his reply. I'm already on my feet and walking in the direction of the bakery's private bathrooms, my heart racing, and my hands all but trembling. Dash affects me, intensely and emotionally. I react to him in a big way that is good and bad. Good in that I'm alive with him, I'm all in with him. Bad in that he can cut me with a word, hurt me without even trying. I turn left down the hallway and then right again, and when I'm finally almost to the sanctuary of the women's room, where I can just pull myself together, Dash is suddenly there, catching my arm and rotating me into him.

"Don't run, Allie," he says, backing me against the door, his big body aligned with mine, his thighs capturing my thighs. I'm angry. I'm aroused by his nearness. I'm angry because I'm aroused when I should only be angry. Even angrier over the whole running thing. "Stop saying that to me."

"You're always one push from being out the door. We just did that. Are we going to do it again?"

"You're pushing now," I say. "That's the point. You *know* *y*ou're pushing me. Is that what you want? Because we both know whatever this is, doesn't fit into your rule book for women."

"The rule book was gone the minute I met you, Allie. And damn straight I'm pushing you, but not away. To be safe."

"It feels like more."

"Because you want it to."

"Because *it is*," I insist.

"No. You're looking for a reason to run."

"Oh my God, stop saying that to me, Dash. Because I'm angry at you does not mean I'm going to run or stop lo—" I catch myself before I confess way too much, before I confess my love for him. What am I doing? I try to deflect from my slip up. "Stop saying that to me."

He reaches around me and opens the door. Before I know his intent, we're inside the tiny bathroom meant for one, and he's locking the door.

LISA RENEE JONES

CHAPTER THIRTY-THREE

"We can't be in here, Dash," I whisper urgently. "Adrianna will be looking for us."

"And yet, we are," he says, his fingers tangling in my hair, tilting my gaze to his as he says, "I'm just making sure you know there's nowhere to run. I'll follow. That's what you've done to me, Allie. That's how much you've taken from me."

"*Taken?*" I demand. "That's what I'm doing?"

"Yeah, baby, but it had to be that way. And I like it. Say what you were going to say. You're not going to stop what?"

"Wanting you."

His lips curve, his breath a warm tease on my lips. "Well just know this, Allie, I won't stop wanting you either."

My God, did we just tell each other we love each other in a public bathroom? "Dash," I whisper. "Dash, what are we doing?"

"This," he says, and his mouth closes down on mine again. And just like that, he's kissing me with such intensity, such passion, I can only moan. I have a vague moment when I realize this is still about control. His control, not my control. The problem is I like it when he's in control. I like his kisses. I like the way his hands feel on my body and when my skirt is at my waist, and only when my skirt is at my waist, do I jolt back to reality. I catch his wrists. "We can't."

"Until we do," he says, cupping my face, kissing me again, Lord help me, his hand is between my legs, pressing under the silk of my panties. His fingers glide through the wet heat of my body and I moan into his mouth. He shocks me then by ripping away my panties. I gasp with the unexpected action, but already he's lifting me, sitting me on top of the bathroom sink. His hands are all over me, and somehow my blouse is open, my bra shoved down, to the point I might as well not be wearing it. His fingers are on my nipples, teasing them, pinching them.

He consumes me oh so easily, but I don't fight it. I'm done resisting.

I reach for him, my hands sliding under his shirt, and we're instantly frenzied, both of us shoving his clothes until his pants are down and he's hot and hard and pressing inside me. Dash scoops my backside, his hands on my now naked backside, and lifts me, folding me into him. Now he's holding both our weights, when he leans against the wall, anchoring us, and I don't even know the person doing this right now.

I'm leaning backward, with nothing but his hand between my shoulder blades holding me up, my breasts thrust in the air, my hips thrust against him and I ride him right here in the bakery bathroom. It's insane. I'm insane. But I don't care. I lose myself in the pleasure, the moment, the man and it's over way too fast but probably not fast enough considering our location. We are fast and hard and wild until we're both panting and I'm leaning into him, my arms wrapping his neck.

Dash shifts our weight and helps me to my feet. Wordlessly, we put our clothes back together before he cups my face and stares down at me. "I'm sorry. I know I pushed hard. I just—I can't—I won't let anything happen to you."

The words "I'm sorry" surprise me, and speak to the many layers that represent this man. The gentle, demanding, intensely talented man who's taken my life by storm. The man who has loved and lost, who can't bear the idea of losing someone else. "I'm sorry, too. I know I scared you. And I do appreciate you worrying about me. But you *did* push hard."

"I don't like Brad Waters' obsession with Allison, that doesn't fit his persona. And I especially don't like that obsession turning on you."

"I don't think that's what's happening." I hug myself. "Is it?"

His hands come on my arms and he says, "We're not taking any chances. Until we find Allison, I want you to be careful. And stop asking around about her. Let Neil— that's my former FBI buddy—do the asking around. Promise me."

"Yes. Of course, I promise. I'm not trying to be stupid. That's why I'm here, where I knew people."

"I shouldn't have used that word. I would never call you stupid. I wasn't calling you stupid." His lips curve and he rubs my cheek. "You have lipstick all over your face. I'll leave you to fix that. I'll be at the table waiting for you. Our table. I'll move your stuff over."

"Our table?"

"Yeah, cupcake. Our table. That okay with you?"

"Yes," I say. "It is."

He strokes my face and when he would turn, when he would leave, I'm overwhelmed with emotion. I catch his arm, halting his exit, and when he looks down at me, I say, "I have no idea why I just stopped you. I just wanted to say something else—"

He cups my face and kisses me. "Yeah. I know. Me, too. But I better go before we get more attention than we need."

I nod and he releases me, exiting the bathroom. I follow him and quickly lock up behind him. My God, what am I doing? Aside from having sex in a public bathroom and almost telling Dash I love him. And I do.

I love Dash Black. I haven't let myself go there, but it's too late. I'm there. I can't turn back and all despite the fact that Dash and I have a cycle starting. We fight, we have sex, we mend. Repeat. Apparently, no matter where we are at the time. And not for the first time, I'm certain that Dash and I are both broken, so very broken.

And I just don't know if we are fixing each other or breaking each other.

CHAPTER THIRTY-FOUR

Cognizant of the time I've been in the bathroom, I quickly mend my face and self-consciously exit the bathroom with hurried steps that lead me to the bakery dining room. And as if having sex in a bathroom, in a place friend's own, isn't transparent enough, there's no discreet way to join Dash because Dash isn't alone. Adrianna is behind the counter, but her dear hubby Jackson is standing by our table, chatting it up with Dash.

Drawing in a calming breath, I close the space between me and them, immediately drawing both men's attention. Dash offers me a sympathetic look and says, "I was telling Jackson here how you tried to put makeup on my eye."

I slide into the seat across from Dash. "I'm not sure he'll believe you considering how bad it looks right now." I glance at Jackson. "Hey, Jackson."

"Hey there, Allie. And yes, indeed. I do believe you failed, missy."

"Yes, well apparently he wears a different shade than me," I say, rolling with the punches better than expected. "Who knew, right?"

Jackson chuckles. "Yes, who knew. But if you're going to let him keep going to that boxing ring, you might better find his shade, too, and keep it on hand." He squeezes Dash's shoulder affectionately. "Talk about keeping the research real, man. Maybe a little too real. I'll get you that coffee and cupcake."

He heads out and leans in closer to Dash. "I swear he has to know."

"Nah," he says, blowing off the concern. "The eye thing worked like a charm. Can you stay here and work with me this afternoon?"

"I wish I could, but it's nuts at the office, the auction is coming together though. In a big way, actually. I need to go back and help Katie, especially if I'm going to New York with you."

His eyes warm with approval. "I want you to go to New York with me so I'll walk you back to the office."

"You stay here and write your book. I'll be fine. It's a short walk."

"I'm walking you," he says stubbornly, standing and calling out to Jackson. "Hold on that order. I'm walking her to the office. I'll be right back."

I don't fight the offer. There are things we need to talk about, some at home when we're alone, and some right now. Dash grabs my coat and helps me put it on, while he sticks with the blazer he's wearing. That Boston blood of his is warm, I guess. We exit to a clean afternoon as a group of kids wearing costumes walk by. There's a pinch in my chest and out of nowhere, I think about having kids with Dash. My God, I'm going too far.

I shove aside the thought and fall into step with Dash. "Your friend—"

"Neil," he supplies.

"Neil," I repeat. "He's really concerned about Allison?"

"Concerned enough to want to dig deeper," he says.

"Should we go to the police?"

"The red tape there is so thick it might as well be stone. Let Neil see what he finds. Give him a few days."

"I know I'm a broken record, but I think something happened to her." I halt and we face each other. "You do, too. That's why Brad didn't sit well with you."

"Obsession that isn't me with you or you with me, doesn't sit well with me."

There is that word again, my thoughts exactly. Is that what this is, I think. *Is that all this is? Obsession?*

"No," he says. "No to whatever you're thinking."

"You don't know what I'm thinking."

"Yes, I do. And no."

We study each other a moment, that battle back at the bakery still between us before we silently turn and start walking again. After a few beats, I shift to another important topic. "How'd it go with Hollywood?"

"There will be a crapload of legal mumbo jumbo, but it looks like we might not even end up with the studio I went to LA to meet. We have multiple bidders, the most appealing is a streaming service. They want me to get involved with the production, for authenticity." He laughs. "Apparently my black eye reminded them of my hands-on experience."

"Oh wow. Well, there's a bright side to all of this, I guess. And what did you say?"

"I don't like LA. *At all.* I don't like the politics of Hollywood, either. But I promised to look at the offer."

"That's exciting," I say. "I mean, Dash. A *TV show*. In today's streaming world that's almost bigger than a movie. Ghost will be happy."

"You have no idea," he says dryly. "As soon as the announcement is made, he'll contact me."

"That's kind of crazy. An assassin will contact you. You don't think he'd ever—"

"Hurt me?" he asks, glancing down at me. "No. I feed his ego and he likes it."

"Yes, well you talked about obsessed," I say as we step to the Hawk Legal front door. "You and Ghost are basically obsessed with each other."

"I'm obsessed with you, baby," he says, sliding a hand to my lower back and leaning in low, near my ear, to whisper. "And I'll be thinking of you in that bathroom all afternoon." He eases back and warm eyes meet mine. "Hurry back. Pick me up in the car. I want to see you behind the wheel." He winks and then he's gone, walking away, headed back to the coffee shop.

I watch him, and all his swagger and confidence, and think again, I love this man. I really love him. I sigh and come back to the present as the back of my neck prickles, as if I'm being watched. Which is crazy. This Allison stuff has me on edge, but it does Dash as well, I think. And that tells me I'm not paranoid. Maybe someone is watching me and I don't like that idea. I turn and hurry inside the building.

CHAPTER THIRTY-FIVE

Once I'm sitting at my desk again with my door shut, I do so with Brad on my mind. That meeting with him *was* odd. And nothing about him sits just right with me. Was he the man in the journal, not Tyler? That question just won't go away. I know I told Dash I would leave this alone right now, but there is a nagging feeling in my gut like I have answers that need to be revealed at my fingertips.

I pull the journal from my purse and stare down at it. I'm not giving this to Neil. It's too personal. And that passage from earlier is bugging me right along with the encounter with Brad. I open to the page I'd read earlier.

I've experienced his touch when it was both punishingly erotic and then when it was a tender caress. I've seen that tenderness in his eyes, as well. I've seen vulnerability in him, too, that no one would believe he's capable of ever experiencing.

There was nothing that resembles this passage in Brad's eyes. Nothing. At all. But she does say that what she saw in the man she's writing about, was not what the rest of the world sees. I flip to the middle of the journal, hoping to get a better tone to where Allison was mentally before she left. This page is titled: *Life after him*

Last night we had a fight, a gut-wrenching, heart-twisting battle, to be more accurate. I did nothing but try to protect him. He just can't cope with me knowing he needs to be protected. He can't allow himself to be openly vulnerable with me. So what did he do? He tried to send me away, then he pulled me back and fucked me senseless. God how he fucked me. But then it was over and the wall crashed back down. It's over. Now it's over.

As for what life is without him. There is none. At least, not one that is happy.

I shiver with the foreboding words certain of one thing. The man in the journal is not Brad. I think it's Tyler.

CHAPTER THIRTY-SIX

The afternoon is just as busy as the morning.

It's one call after another, but I decide that going to New York, and Riptide, is a good idea. The generous donations come with a huge challenge. Can we get them validated in time? The real possibility that we cannot means we might auction items off for too little. And to rush the validations is expensive in itself, and I don't know if Riptide, Mark specifically, will allow that to happen. I pull up my email and shoot him a note:

Mr. Compton—

The generosity of donations for this auction is astounding. The items donated by country music royalty are dream-worthy. The problem is that each item needs validation. I just don't have the time and manpower. I'm thinking of coming there at the end of the month to try to figure it all out. I could really use your expert advice. I'm in over my head but trying to swim to the surface and make this a win for all involved, especially Riptide.

Looking forward to your input,

Allie

Once the email is sent, I send Katie home. It's five after all. She can work from home, which is what I intend as well. I text Dash: *On my way. You want to work there a while or go home?*

Home, baby, he replies. *How do you feel about Chinese food?*

Hungry, I text back. *I'll pull to the door, but you're driving us home.*

Home.

We are having the kind of conversations that only couples have. It's really kind of surreal. My computer beeps with a message from Mark. I quickly pull it up to read:

Ms. Wright—

Since you work here, and you're reporting to the wrong office, having you show up to the right one for a change would be appreciated. As for the quandary you're in, I have answers. I'll share those answers when you show up to work.

Goodnight.

The message is so very Mark Compton. While some might think he's reprimanding me, I'm fairly certain he just told me that I'm missed. It's nice to be missed. It's confusing to be missed. The push and pull between New York and Nashville is real.

For now, though, I have Nashville on my mind.

I gather my things, and with my briefcase loaded up and on my shoulder, I decide to stop by Tyler's office yet again. I've tried to catch up with him twice earlier, in the hopes of talking about New York, but he's been nowhere to be found. And his secretary is no help. She just blinks at me and says, "He's not in."

I exit the lobby to find the doors to Tyler's side of the office locked with the lights out. Okay then, so much for that. Honestly, the whole place is a ghost town at only five o'clock. I step into the elevator and it's not long before I'm in the parking garage. I step out of the car and freeze with the utter silence. No one is around and I curse Dash for making me so jumpy. That prickly sensation on the back of my neck is back and I grab the car keys from my purse and scan the area. I see no one, but I feel someone. Or now, I really am going crazy.

I start walking, and when I get to the car, despite clicking the unlock button on the key, it's not unlocked.

BECAUSE I CAN

I try again. It won't unlock. I want to scream. I'm about to call Dash when a fancy sportscar pulls into the spot two cars over. I'm relieved for the company and determined to be in the car before whoever just arrived heads inside and I'm alone with whoever my stalker is again. Not that I really have a stalker. I just keep feeling like I'm being watched. At this point I set my bag on the ground, and right when I would dial Dash, Tyler is standing beside me, looking so very arrogantly handsome, and perfectly *him,* in a blue pinstriped suit.

"Problems, Ms. Wright?"

"I can't get the car to unlock," I reluctantly admit, my cheeks heating. "As silly as that sounds. It's not even the first time I drove this car."

He holds out a commanding hand. I offer him the keys. He clicks the lock. "Try it now."

I open the door. "Okay, I'm embarrassed. How did you do that?"

"The new M4's have a tricky key. Which you don't know because it's not your car." He holds out the key for me to take.

I close my hand around them but he doesn't let go. "When your identity becomes his identity, what is left of you, Ms. Wright?"

Unexpectedly, he doesn't hit a nerve, nor does he stir insecurity in me, as I might expect with this remark. This is now, I refuse to allow Tyler to muddy the water of past and present. Nor will he force a reply that would be about my mistakes, someone that is not Dash.

"Allie," I correct defiantly. "Ms. Wright is as generic as you accuse me of becoming. And I'm not losing my identity to Dash. I'm borrowing his car. Mine broke down."

He studies me a moment and releases the keys. "You realize he's not a simple man, I assume?"

"I'm pretty sure we're both clear on that point," I say, my defensiveness for Dash driving me to add, "but rarely are brilliant, creative people simple."

"He's got demons chasing him," he says. "You either accept those demons or you walk away. And if you walk away, do it now, not later, when you do so bleeding."

"I don't choose to accept his demons. I choose to help him fight them."

"And you think you can do what no one else can?"

"Is that what happened with Allison, Tyler?" I ask before I can stop myself. "Did she try and help you fight your demons and the demons won?"

His lips thin. "You, Ms. Wright, never know your limits. And you *do* have limits."

"As do you, just the wrong ones." I'm speaking of the journal entries, of course, of his unwillingness to be vulnerable with Allison.

He arches a brow. "Meaning what?"

"Nothing. I have limits, remember?" I change the subject. "But speaking of limits, the donations have been generous, but I don't know if I can get all the validations done in time for the auction. We need to get to pricing. I need to go to New York City and go through the auction validations in person. If they can even get them all done. They are volunteering their help."

His intelligent blue eyes narrow on me and his lips curve slightly. "Let me guess. You'd like to go during Dash's charity signing."

I don't justify that remark with a counter punch. I simply say, "Yes. A few days before so I have plenty of time at Riptide."

"Offer Riptide a commission on anything they validate and sell." With that, he turns and starts walking. I draw in a breath and call after him.

"Tyler."

He halts and turns to face me. "Yes, Ms. Wright?"

"Tell her you love her, leave it on her machine, text her, but mean it. Go in all the way. If you do that and she's okay, she'll come back for you."

He inhales sharply and then says nothing. He just turns and starts walking.

LISA RENEE JONES

CHAPTER THIRTY-SEVEN

I pull up to the bookstore and I'm out of the car as soon as the engine is idling. Dash is joining me in a quick flash and I hand him the keys. "You don't want to drive me home, cupcake?"

"Tyler had to unlock the car for me, so no. When I can't even open the doors, I should not be trusted behind the wheel."

He laughs a low, sexy laugh and helps me into my side of the car, kissing me soundly on the lips before heading around to the driver's side. "Sorry, baby," he says, joining me. "The key glitches. I should have given you a few tips, but you seemed to have the swing of things."

"Well, how could you know I can't operate a basic door? On the positive side, I told him about New York."

His eyes light with mischief. "Told him?"

"Actually, yes. I did."

That evening, Dash and I order our Chinese food, and eat and work upstairs in the bedroom sitting area, while the sun sets. It's a good night that neither one of us seems eager to spoil with outside influences. We don't talk about Tyler. We don't talk about Allison. We keep things about us. When it's finally time to throw in the towel on work, Dash takes our leftovers downstairs. I grab my shoes from the floor and walk to the closet to figure out what to wear tomorrow since I haven't taken anything to the cleaners, only to find shopping bags all over the floor of my closet. I drop my shoes and kneel down, peeking inside a bag that holds a pair of Chanel dress pants. The next bag is lingerie. My eyes catch on the garment bags hanging next to my clothes. I stand up and go to them, unzipping one of them to find a gorgeous pink Chanel dress.

"I looked at your labels and sizes," Dash says from the doorway. "I tried to get as much right as I could."

I whirl around to face him. "What is this, Dash?"

"It's a big closet. I wanted to fill it for you, but you can take anything you don't want back."

I fight the triggers that want to consume me. My father bought me gifts. Brandon bought me gifts. They had a plan and it was to own me, in a way no one could believe possible, actually. A horrible, embarrassing plan. It's why I don't own those gifts now. Just the bag I kept to remind me of exactly who, and what, my father is.

"I don't claim to be an expert shopper, at all," Dash adds. "In fact, I've never shopped for anyone but my sister."

I blink him into view. "You did this yourself? You actually went and shopped for me?"

"Yes. Well, the salespeople helped me, but none of us know your taste. But I also knew you wouldn't let me take you shopping either. So, take anything you don't like back, baby."

I let the garment bag in my hand slide away and swallow hard, tears welling in my eyes. "Hey, hey, hey," Dash says, stepping over bags to join me, cupping my face and stroking my cheek. "What just happened? I was trying to make you happy, not sad."

"I was about to turn all of this down, but then you said you shopped for me. You did this."

"Why would you turn down the gifts, Allie?" he asks softly.

"I told you I'm not about the money, Dash. And I make my own money. You don't have to support me."

"Is that how you look at this?" His hands settle on my shoulders. "Me supporting you? That's not what this is.

I don't buy gifts for women, Allie. Never. It's not my thing. But hell, I take that back. I am taking care of you. I want you to have nice things. What is wrong with that?"

"Nothing," I say. "I appreciate what you did. The idea of you shopping for me is honestly swoon-worthy, Dash. But from now on, after this, I want you, just you, not what you can buy me. Don't you want to know that I'm here for you?"

"I already know you're here for me, Allie. You going to tell me what this is all about? Is it about your father?"

"He has a history of fancy gifts and broken promises." I grab his waist. "I know that's not you. I just want us to be real."

He strokes my hair. "Baby, we're as real as it gets. Take the clothes. Enjoy them. Trade them in for things you love. Hopefully, I did good on a few things."

"The pink dress. I already love it. And the lingerie—"

"Is for me," he says.

I smile and he reaches in his pocket and produces a credit card. "I want you to take this."

I hold up my hands. "No. No, that I'm not taking."

"I want you to have it. And use it. I paid off your mother's medical bills today."

"Medical bills?" I pulled back to study him. "What medical bills?"

"I saw the stack of bills when I was there."

"I don't understand. She has great insurance."

"Even with good insurance, her portion was hefty."

"How much, Dash?"

"Fifty thousand."

"Oh my God." My hands press together. "Oh my God. You paid off a fifty-thousand-dollar bill?"

"Yeah, baby, but she doesn't know. I did it anonymously."

"Oh my God," I say because I can't seem to say anything else. "I have twenty thousand in savings. I'll write you a check. And Riptide offered me a bonus and—" I try to move around him and he catches me to him.

"It's done, baby. I got this. And I got you."

"You are too generous, Dash. I don't even know how to take this from you."

"By just doing it." He presses the card in my hand. "Just so I know if you need anything you have it." I open my mouth to speak and he says, "Humor me. Keep it in your purse. Please."

"Okay," I say. My fingers curl on his chest. "No one has ever done anything like this for me, Dash. Not like this."

He cups my face and tilts my gaze to his. "And no one has ever been quite like you, cupcake. You have a good mother. We'll take care of her. Together."

"We have to go see her before we leave for New York."

"I'm in. Whenever you want."

"Dinner tomorrow night?"

"Dinner tomorrow night works."

He kisses me. "Check out your new clothes. I'll bang out a few more words. And, Allie?"

"Yes?"

"Nothing. We'll talk in bed."

I smile. "We won't talk in bed."

"No," he says with a smile. "We won't talk in bed. But we'll try."

He leaves me in the closet, and I turn and stare at all the bags everywhere. He is good to me and it's not with an agenda. He is just good to me. He wants to do this for me. I step out of the doorway and into the bedroom, calling after Dash.

"Dash."

He rotates to face me. "Yeah, baby?"

"How will you know I'm here for you? Not all of this?"

He closes the space between us and says, "The same way you know I didn't try and buy you like your father. You'll know. And I'll know." And then he's kissing me, undressing me, and we end up in the bed. Where we prove our prediction one hundred percent correct. We do *not* talk.

LISA RENEE JONES

CHAPTER THIRTY-EIGHT

The next morning, I dress in my new pink Chanel dress with a pleated skirt, that looks like it belongs in Vogue. It's my first "new" Chanel anything. I'm checking myself in the mirror when Dash appears behind me. "You like it?"

"I love it," I say, glancing over my shoulder and up at him.

"Hmmm," he says, wrapping an arm around me and nuzzling my neck. "Me, too, but I think I'd like it better on the floor."

I rotate to face him. "I have to get to work. You know that. I have a couple of the firm's clients coming in to talk about their donations this morning."

He groans but releases me. "For the good of the cause, I'll wait to undress you until later."

I'm smiling an hour later when I claim my desk for the day, and quickly call my mother. "Mother," I greet when she answers.

"Daughter," she replies.

I smile at the formality of our little game we play often on the phone. "Will you make me your famous pot pie tonight?"

She laughs. "You want me to slave in the kitchen for you, do you?"

"Yep. That's what I want."

"Are you bringing that handsome man of yours?"

"Actually, I am. And so I don't forget to tell you, we're going to New York a few days before Halloween."

"*We're*? As in you and Dash?"

"Yes. As in me and Dash mom."

"You two are getting quite close it seems."

"Well, yes. I guess on that note, I should tell you that I moved in with him."

"What?" she says. "You did—you—wow. Does this mean you're staying in Nashville?"

"I'm trying not to overthink it."

"January is soon, honey. I'm not sure that's overthinking."

"I have at least a month to six weeks before I have to make a big decision."

"I'm pretty sure you already did. You moved in with him. That's already a big decision."

"You don't approve?"

"Oh, I like that young man. So does your stepfather. Just be careful. The heart can be a delicate flower, and he's a high-profile, famous man. I won't judge all by one, but I certainly got burned by someone of that caliber."

"He's not like him," I promise her, a knot forming in my belly just thinking of how badly my father hurt her.

"No," she agrees. "I don't believe he is, but both of you need to earn each other's trust."

"Wise advice from a wise woman."

"Yeah, yeah," she says. "I'll make your pot pie. Bring him on over here. I'm going to inspect him with a keener eye this time. Feel free to warn him. Be here at six."

I'm laughing when we hang up. I'm happy, I realize. I've been challenged, engaged, motivated, angry, inspired, and the list goes on, but I don't remember the last time I was happy. I reach inside my desk where I've stashed the journal and pick it up, thinking about how many times and ways I've compared myself to Allison. I've been curious why she would leave a dream job, but I suddenly understand. It's about a bigger picture, about where you feel you are and where you belong. Anyone looking in on me would wonder why I would leave Riptide. The answer is happiness. The people we love are the sunshine on even the rainiest day. We need them. They are bonds that hold us together in the stormiest of days.

I wonder if anywhere in the writing on these pages, Allison ever said she was happy. I slide the journal back into my purse without looking at it. I already know the answer. She wasn't happy. And right now, I really want to believe she chose to leave to find her sunshine.

LISA RENEE JONES

CHAPTER THIRTY-NINE

It's five-thirty when Dash calls my phone. "I'm in the parking garage."

"I'm coming right down," I say and I waste no time doing just that.

I step off the elevator expecting him and his M4 to greet me. Instead, Dash is leaning on a burgundy car I've never seen, one booted foot over the other. It's Dash I'm focused on though and not the car. How can I not notice him first? He's in faded jeans, a brown sweater, and a brown leather jacket and he is sin and hot sex in bakery bathrooms.

I close the space between us and he pushes off the car, pulling me close, and kissing me. "This is why I went shopping. I get to look at you in all the new clothes."

"You, Mr. Black, know all the right things to say. I guess that's why you're a writer."

"Depends on which critic you ask, baby. Some say I should have stuck to the FBI." He holds up a key. "Your car."

"You didn't have to rent me a car. It is a rental, right?"

"Something like that," he says, noncommittally. "Check it out." He grabs my bag and I bring the car fully into focus. "It's a BMW. That's an expensive rental, Dash."

"I have a thing for BMW," he says. "A bit like you do Chanel."

"It's beautiful, but how much is this costing?"

"That means the dealership likes me. *A lot.* I worked out a deal. You drive us to your mom's. Make sure you like it."

"I already love it. It's gorgeous," I say. "And the color is very me." I push to my toes and kiss his cheek. "I'd tell you it's too much, but I know how you'd reply." I soften my voice. "Thank you."

"Anything for you, cupcake." He gives me one of his most charming smiles and opens the driver's door for me.

It's right then that Tyler steps off the elevator and walks right for us, or rather, Dash. Tyler stops right in front of him. "I hear Ghost is going to a streaming service."

"We'll see," Dash replies. "Negotiations are ongoing."

"They want you. They'll pay what it takes. You're about to be an even richer man than you already are." He eyes me. "Don't get lost in the fireworks, Ms. Wright." With that, he steps around us and heads to his car.

In other words, don't lose my identity. "What did that mean?" Dash asks, facing me now, and me him.

"He warned me about you. He said you have demons."

"And you said?"

"Now they're my demons, too."

He catches the top of the open door with his hand. "I don't know if that's a good thing, Allie. Maybe that makes me a selfish fuck."

I press my hand to his cheek, his light brown, one-day stubble, teasing my palm. "No. It makes you human. And I love that about you."

It's as close to telling him I love him as I've come. If he notices, he doesn't show it. He covers my hands with his and kisses my knuckles. "Climb in, baby. We need to get to your mom's."

It's not what he wants to say to me. I feel that. But I don't know that right here, in the Hawk Legal parking lot, he can say much more. I slide into the leather seat, and then to my surprise, Dash kneels beside me. "One day you're going to leave me. And just know this, I don't want you to leave, Allie."

I open my mouth to reply, but already he's standing, and shutting me inside the car. He slides in beside me and says, "Rev her up and let's see how she drives."

Obviously, he doesn't want to talk about why I might leave him. He wants me to let this go. And so, I do. For now. I let it go. But I'm not letting him go. I've learned something about Dash tonight, something I already knew but let myself forget. He goes and encourages people to beat him up in the ring because he hates himself. And I don't know why. Not yet. And I don't think he wants me to know why.

CHAPTER FORTY

My mother greets us at the door and we've barely stepped into the hallway when she flings her arms around Dash. "Thank you. I know what you did, Dash Black. Thank you." And then she bursts into tears. "You have no idea the pressure we were feeling and I didn't want to tell Allie. I didn't want to worry her." She looks up at Dash with absolute gratitude beaming from her eyes. "And don't tell me it wasn't you. The only other person in my life with money is my ex, and he would never help me."

"Well, I will," Dash promises her. "Always."

"I can't believe he did this," my mother says, hugging me now. "How did he know?"

Dash and my stepfather have moved down the hallway now toward the kitchen. "He saw some bills when he was here. He did this for you before he told me. And he didn't want the credit. He just wanted to help."

"My God, Allie. I've never known someone so generous and kind."

"Funny, but that's not how he sees himself at all."

"Well, then he needs you to change that. You know that, right?"

"Yes, Mom. I do. Very much."

We join the men in the kitchen, and Dash slides an arm around me. For the next hour, we laugh and chat, and my mother goes nuts over Dash's TV news. "What about Henry Cavill as Ghost?" she suggests.

"She wants Henry Cavill to be in everything," my stepfather says dryly.

"And you want Kate Beckinsale."

Dash and I laugh at their exchange, and he good-naturedly plays along with their casting suggestions.

It's a good evening and when Dash and I step outside, I want more than anything to tell him how much I love him. But I don't want him to think it's an emotional response to my mother's emotional response. So I don't tell him. Not now.

"Can you drive?" I ask.

"Of course," he says, walking me to the passenger side of the car.

He opens my door and I step into him. "She says you're the most generous, kind person she's ever known."

"And what did you say?"

"That you don't see yourself that way."

"How do you think I see myself, Allie?"

"Broken like me."

There is something jagged and dark that flickers in his eyes. "Broken, but not like you. Let's go home."

I climb inside the car, and I know that all of his broken pieces, and mine, too, want to cut us. I don't want to let that happen. I just don't know if it can be stopped. It's as if we're glued together, perhaps by each other, but it's only so long until we shatter.

CHAPTER FORTY-ONE

The next few days, Dash and I start forming little habits together. When we workout, who makes the coffee—me, usually—and a meetup for lunch, which for now, is at the bookstore, which seems to be his best writing location. Meanwhile, I start feeling like the auction is coming together. It's on the evening before Dash and I leave for New York, that I step onto the elevator to find myself alone with Tyler's father.

"Mr. Hawk," I say, surprised to find him here and I don't know why. He's the center of everything here at Hawk Legal. "How are you?" I ask, out of a lack of any more brilliant conversation piece.

"Jack," he corrects, turning to face me as I follow his lead and do the same of him.

That's when I really look at him, his piercing gray eyes intimidatingly observant. Not to mention, it really is astounding how much he looks like Tyler—tall, athletic, and good-looking, though there is something about Hawk senior that is calculating in a way I do not read from Tyler. Hence the intimidating observant eyes.

"Jack," I amend.

"Better," he approves. "And as to the question, how am I? I'm quite wonderful, thank you. How are you? I hear you're making us look good with this charity auction."

He's heard. From Tyler, I assume, which is curious. The two of them don't exactly get along, so I wonder how any conversation between them goes anyplace but badly. "I'm certainly trying," I say. "I'm headed to New York to coordinate the appraisals of the auction items tomorrow actually."

"At Riptide, correct? Isn't that where you worked before joining us?"

"Technically," I say, "I still do. I'm on leave until January."

"In other words," he observes, "my son hasn't convinced you to stay as of yet."

"Not exactly," I say. "It's complicated."

The elevator opens and he motions me forward. We now have the awkward walk to the garage elevator. Together. This encounter just won't end and as if proving that point, the minute we're in the second elevator, Jack is facing me again. "Define complicated."

"I never intended to stay," I reply, "and now the question of staying or going, becomes, as I said, complicated."

"Ah," he says. "Complicated is personal. I understand."

The doors open and I all but bolt into the garage, eager to escape to my car, but he's not having it. He steps into my space and pauses beside me. "Perhaps I can make it less complicated, *Allie*. We'll talk when you get back from New York."

He gives me a warm look, almost too warm, though I feel as if Jack Hawk flirts with the world, it's just his way before he walks toward what I believe to be a Jaguar. Once I'm in my car, I replay the conversation. What exactly does that mean? He's going to make it less complicated?

And why does it make me uncomfortable?

CHAPTER FORTY-TWO

Dash books us in first class for the long flight to New York City, and does so with the hopes he can get in some good quality writing time. It's mid-day when we settle into our seats and I'm a bit emotional about the trip.

The flight attendant offers us drinks and Dash orders some sort of whiskey while I welcome a glass of champagne. .3

"You're nervous," Dash observes.

"Why do you say that?"

"I'm observant like that. Talk to me. What are you feeling?"

"Excited for your signing. Nervous about dealing with my boss."

"Why nervous?"

"Well, if you knew Mark Compton, you'd understand that he creates that in everyone. But bottom line, he's going to pressure me about my loyalty to Riptide over Hawk Legal."

"And where does it lie?"

With you, and my mother, I think, *but also to the job I'm tasked with performing.* "To the charity," I say. "I'm passionate about what I'm doing with it. I want it to be wildly successful."

"I'm glad you are," he says, and it feels as if he's talking about more than my commitment to the charity. Almost as if he knows that commitment is part of my commitment to him.

"Didn't you say you've traveled with your job?" he asks.

"I went to Germany, London, and Italy, and a couple of different states, all for publishing events."

"And you liked those places?"

"Italy and Germany quite a lot. I didn't get to see much of London. The event was just too far from the tourist sites."

"London is a lot like New York City, familiar in a way you don't expect. Did you ever travel with your father?"

"No," I say. "He was literally gone my entire childhood. My understanding is he left my mom behind when he went on the road. It made it easier to play around on her. When I first got the job in publishing, she was jealous. Books and travel were as much her dream job as mine."

"Good thing you like both considering books and travel are my life. I'm pretty sure we can find some ways to turn her into an adventurer."

"Dash," I whisper, my heart squeezing with his words that suggest we are so much more than a three-month playdate. His eyes meet mine, tenderness in their depths, as he lifts my hand and kisses it.

The moment is cut short when the intercom sounds and announcements are made, forcing us to prepare for takeoff. "You need to write," I say. "We both know you're going to get pressured about that book in New York."

"Yeah. You have no idea, baby. But yes, I'm going to write."

We settle back into our seats, and I rest my head on the cushion. I'm going to New York with Dash, which in and of itself, is really quite surreal. But even more so how I feel about my return to the city. It's hard to believe that the city of lights, action, and magic that it had once been to me, is more a muted story that feels overdone.

CHAPTER FORTY-THREE

After a flight delay and dinner in the airport, we arrive at the Jersey airport at eight that night. By the time we're in Manhattan, it's after nine. By the time we're in the fancy presidential suite of a high-rise hotel, we're halfway to ten. The bellman escorts us to our room, and while Dash talks to him, I take in the room of blues and creams that includes a living area kitchen combo, and a full dining table. Of course, there are windows. Lots of windows, with the kind of views that only the rich and famous enjoy in this city.

Dash's money and power, as well as his fame, is everywhere, much like my father's money, power, and fame. Perhaps that should scare me, sending me running all over again. But it doesn't. Those things don't define Dash's character as anything close to my father's. Dash is a man who can be confident but not arrogant, blessed and therefore generous, gifted, and yet humble. My father is his polar opposite.

The door shuts behind me and when I would rave about how pretty it is here, Dash is pulling me into his arms, folding me close, his hand on the back of my head. "In case I haven't told you, I'm glad you're here with me, Allie." His mouth closes down on mine and with what I can only call a wicked sweet heat that sweeps over us, and consumes the very air around us.

He scoops my backside and lifts me, my legs wrapping his waist as he carries me to the living area, and sets me down in front of the couch.

We undress each other then, no words spoken, but there is a tenderness between us that I have never quite felt before, a shift, a growing intimacy. And when he sits down and pulls me on top of him, straddling his hips, when he's inside me, pressed deeply, I know that we are making love, perhaps really making love for the first time ever. I ride him with a slow sway of my hips, and his eyes and hands are somehow hungry, and yet, there is a tenderness to every moment we share. And when I collapse on top of him, my face buried in his neck, my breasts pressed to his chest, I don't want to move. I want to stay just like this for the rest of the night. And I know now that Dash and I are not two ships passing in the night. We are two ships sailing together, navigating stormy waters, but finding the calm with each other.

CHAPTER FORTY-FOUR

The next morning, I dress in a multi-toned, form-fitting pencil skirt and a silk blouse while Dash is the cool, confident writer in jeans, boots, and a sleek, tan leather jacket. And he makes it work. He owns the look. He owns the room. He owns *me*, I think. Most definitely me. Once we step outside the hotel into a biting wind, I decide Nashville, even during an unusual cold spell, is not even close to this bitter. Dash and the driver escort me to Riptide, where Dash walks me to the door. "I'll only be a few hours. Then I'll come and get you?"

"Yes. Perfect. I don't need more than a few hours."

His fingers close around my waist, under the Burberry trenchcoat I'm wearing, and he walks me to him. "You look beautiful today."

My cheeks heat despite the cold wind. "Thank you," I say softly.

"I'll show you how beautiful in a few hours."

With that promise, he kisses me and opens the door to Riptide. I hurry inside and I'm greeted first by the security guard, and then by the receptionist. Many other greetings follow, but my path is a straight shot to Mark's office. I stop at his door and knock, peeking inside. He sits behind his desk, a combination of good looks and absolute control of all things around him, that no one would deny. He's present. He owns the room.

He motions me forward and I claim the seat in front of his desk. "You're glowing, Ms. Wright. Nashville has done right by you. Why do I believe that means you are not going to do right by me?"

"I would never do wrong by you, Mark."

"Leaving is doing wrong by me."

"Nothing has changed as of now. I'll be back in January."

He arches a brow. "As of now?"

"It's hard to leave my mother, but she's healthy now. There's no reason I should hang on so tightly. How is your mother?"

"She's a fighter," he says tightly, offering nothing more. But of course, he wouldn't. This is, after all, the stoic, Mr. Compton.

"If she would like to talk to my mother, another cancer survivor, and a nurse, I can connect them."

His expression, even his shoulders, visibly soften in an unfamiliar way, for such a hard man, his mother's illness continuing to offer just a hint of something gentler beneath his surface. "Yes. I do believe she could use an ear and voice from someone who understands what she'd gone through."

"Of course. I love your mom. And my mom. I think they will connect in a positive way. I'll make it happen."

"Tell me about the auction," he says, his tone turning hard again.

"You got my message about Hawk Legal paying you for rush validations?"

"I did. We'll donate the time and energy for the press, and for a promise of your return."

He'll donate the services for me? I blinked, shocked at such a generous offer. "To work here has been a dream," I say. "To be valued here, an honor, but he'll pay you," I say quickly. "Take the money, Mr. Compton. Please."

"In other words, you're not coming back."

"Nothing has changed. My plans are the same as when I left."

"And yet, Ms. Wright, it has. You have. I can see that in your eyes. You need to look in the mirror and see it, too. Then, make your decision and own it." He leans back. "I'll donate the services because I believe you'll make this auction a win for everyone involved. Now go figure out how you win, Ms. Wright."

I stand and leave his office, and when I return to mine, it doesn't feel like mine anymore.

***

Dash has meetings run over into the late afternoon which ends up working out just fine, considering I'm far from done here at Riptide. It's five when I join Dash in the back of the hired SUV.

"We have just enough time to grab a bite at the hotel restaurant before cocktails with the publisher. I want you to come with me."

"Which publisher? The one I worked for or your new publisher?"

"The one you worked for. Since they published all the books currently released, they're overseeing the signing."

"Drinks with both of our ex-employers. This should be loads of fun," I say sarcastically. "How can I not want to attend?"

He laughs and gives me one of his devastating smiles. "Better with you, than without you, baby. Of that, I'm certain."

I smile with him now and decide that coming to New York was a good thing for me. I'm facing the past with the man who may well be my future. And if I decide to leave that past behind, I will walk away. I will not run.

CHAPTER FORTY-FIVE

Turns out cocktails are not just cocktails.

We arrive at the restaurant to discover the publisher has rented out the entire place. "I'm going to kill Bella," Dash says, reading a text from her. "She thought she told me this was a big deal tonight." He slides his phone into his pocket. "Sorry, baby, but now we become the show. And I mean we. You up for this?"

"Riptide events are one big press event," I say. "I'm well-practiced."

"You're going as my woman, Allie. There will be photos. There will be talk."

"Well, in hindsight I wish I would have changed clothes, but yeah, I get it. All photos that get posted will probably be ones of me with my mouth open, or falling over my own feet, and the speculation about me will have tongues wagging."

"You sure you want to do this?"

"Do *you* want me to do this?" I counter.

"I do," he says. "And I promise to catch you if you fall over your own feet."

"Unless I take you down with me."

"That could be fun," he teases and opens the door.

A few minutes later, we're in a three-level bar with fancy drop lights and dark décor. Dash and I are greeted by his former editor and my ex-boss. Ellen is tall, thin, attractive, and in her mid-fifties. She greets Dash with eagerness and gives me a wide-eyed inspection. "Allie."

"Hi, Ellen, good to see you."

"How did you get here tonight? Are you back in publishing?"

Dash slides his arm around me. "With me."

LISA RENEE JONES

Ellen blanches. "Oh—I—Well. That's an interesting pairing. You both do love books."

"Yes, we do," Dash says. "And we both need a drink."

"Yes, get a drink and enjoy yourself," she says. "I was made aware of a few things we need to address before the singing. Can we meet in the morning?"

"Just call me," Dash says. "I have a book I'm trying to crunch." Dash directs me away from her, and says, "Drinks. Now."

I laugh and say, "I better not or I'll be your drunk party date and that won't look good."

"Hmm. It's not called drunk. At these kinds of parties, it's called sane."

We manage to get our drinks and claim a standing bar table before Dash is suffocated in attention, but attention he does get. One after another, people come up to him and he signs more than a few books. There's a slight break in the crowd of people forming around our standing bar table when my gaze locks with another's across the room and my lips part. Brandon. Brandon is here.

Bodies move and my view of his location is suddenly blocked. I shift and lean left and right, but when the place he was standing is cleared, he's not there. Did I imagine him? Yes. Of course, I imagined him. Why would he be here? He has nothing to do with Dash and Dash's books. *No more booze for me*, I think, setting aside the half glass of champagne I have left. This is me looking in the mirror, as Mark said, and feeling shame. I'm embarrassed about being used and made a fool. Being back here, among the people I worked with when it all came raining down, must be stirring up the ghosts of my past.

A reporter steps to the table across from us and focuses on Dash, of course. "I'm Connor Meyers from

188

Men's Health Magazine. We'd really like to profile you. I've got a call into your agent to try and seal that deal."

I lean in and whisper, "Bathroom," to Dash, and then slide away from the table.

Turns out there's a line, and I decide to try the second level. I might get done and back sooner. Sure enough, upstairs, a few people mingle about, but the real crowd is downstairs with Dash. I walk down a hallway by the bar, and enter the bathroom, quickly do my thing, wash up, and then stare into the mirror. What do I see? *Not the same woman I was with Brandon,* I think. But Brandon is devious, vicious, a man who will lash out. Which means, now that I'm in the press with Dash, I have to warn Dash.

The past is only the past when you face it in the future. I read that in a book. No truer words have been written.

Resolved to do what is right, I open the bathroom door and go cold. Brandon is standing there, waiting on me. I wasn't imagining him. He's tall, dark, handsome, with a John Travolta dimple in his chin, that I once thought attractive. Now I can barely look at him. "What are you doing here?"

"I was invited."

Alarm bells are chiming in my head, warning me that he's up to something. "You have no vested interest in Dash's books."

"You underestimate my reach, Allie, sweetheart. You always did." He steps into me, presses a hand on the wall. "Your father dumped me when you left me. I don't suggest you underestimate me now."

In other words, he's after payback. "Step away," I hiss. "Get away from me." His hand comes down on my waist and I shove his chest. "Damn it, Brandon, I'll scream."

Suddenly, Dash is there, pushing Brandon back and stepping toe-to-toe with him. "Who are you and what the hell do you think you're doing?"

I grab Dash's arm, holding onto him. "Dash let's walk away. Let's go, *now*. I'll explain."

"Dash Black," Brandon greets. "I hear you like to punch things. You going to punch me now?"

My heart is racing, charging a million miles an hour. Does he know about the fight club? Dash's lips curve, and not kindly. "What's the fun of hitting someone who'll just fall down?"

"I assure you, I won't fall down. I'll rise to the challenge." Brandon smirks and to my surprise, actually walks away.

The minute he's gone I turn to Dash and just start spewing information. "Oh my God, Dash. That's Brandon. My ex. He's an agent, he was my father's agent. My father dropped him over me and he wants me to pay. He wants to hurt you to hurt me. And he knows about your fighting."

"Easy, baby." He maneuvers me around the corner, down a second hallway leading to the men's bathroom, and turns me to face him, his hands on my shoulders. "He knows what the press told him. I just had a black eye from a sparring session. He wanted me to hit him so he could get a payday. That's all."

"You don't know him like I do. He's resourceful. He's devious. I need you to understand how devious. I overheard him telling someone I was his cash cow. He was marrying me for my dad's money and my dad knew. He gave him the stamp of approval. My father wanted me away from my mother's influence, because she kept me hating him. He wanted the money. Now I didn't just take that from him, my father fired him. And God, this is so embarrassing."

190

Dash slides one hand between my shoulder blades and molds me close, the other holds my head. "Do not be embarrassed with me, Allie. God, woman, I love you so fucking much, you don't ever have to be embarrassed."

I blink, stunned, all kinds of crazy emotions flooding my entire body. "You love me?"

He tilts my head back, looks into my eyes, and says, "So fucking much and I don't want you to come back to New York." His mouth closes down on mine in a kiss I feel to my toes, a kiss that is so much more than a kiss. It's passion, it's friendship, it's love.

"I love you, too," I whisper, when his lips part mine. "And I want to stay with you." He strokes my hair from my eyes and says, "Let's get out of here."

"Can you?"

"Hell yeah, baby." He closes his hand around mine and leads me to the door.

Once we're in the back of the hired SUV, he pulls me to him and kisses me again, and by the time we're in the hotel room, we are combustible. We never make it past the front door. We're naked in about sixty seconds, and I'm against the door while he presses inside me, thrusting and pumping, while I pant through the pleasure.

When we collapse on the floor, we both laugh at the fact that we are literally naked and sitting against the front door. "You want to try the bedroom next?"

"You think we should talk first?"

"I know all I need to know. He lost you. You're mine now."

"Dash, really? He's a problem."

He stands and pulls me to my feet. "And I haven't fucked you well enough or you would not be naked and talking about another man. Challenge accepted." He scoops me up and carries me toward the bedroom.

CHAPTER FORTY-SIX

The next day, Dash dresses casually for a day working in the hotel. I dress in a black skirt and teal blouse with the intention of working at Riptide for a few hours.

"The driver will be here to get you in twenty minutes," Dash says as I join him at the dining table for room service coffee and pastries.

I accept the coffee he pours me and decide that passion and midnight go together. So do daylight and reality. That reality is punching me in the face. "Brandon is going to come for you to hurt me, Dash."

"I'll have Bella dig around and find out why he was at the party," he promises. "We're working in the same circles. It's possible he just happened to be there."

"You're underestimating him, Dash."

"Don't underestimate me, baby. I got this. And I told you, I got you."

He offers me the creamer and I accept, wishing there was some way to get Dash to really take Brandon seriously.

"Hey," he says, drawing my gaze to his.

"I heard you loud and clear. I'm not a man without resources, Allie. I will handle him. I need you to trust me enough to know that when I say that, I mean it."

Because he's ex-FBI, I remind myself.

His cellphone buzzes and he glances at the message. "That's the driver. He's here early but he can wait."

"I'll just go on down. The sooner I get to work, the sooner I get back." I push to my feet.

Dash follows and folds me close, cupping my face. "Considering what that asshole did to you, you trusting me, is a big order, I know. But I'm not him, baby."

"I do trust you, Dash. The problem is, the only thing I trust about Brandon is his ability to do bad things to serve his own greater good."

"And he's not the first Brandon I've dealt with. He's nothing next to Ghost, I promise you."

"I try not to think about Ghost hanging around and watching us. Is he? Watching us?"

"Try not to think about it." He teases. "Then again, maybe you should think of Ghost, not Brandon. On another subject, I want to set a service to move your apartment before we leave. You okay with that?"

"You're not letting me back out, are you?"

"Not a chance. Do you want to back out?"

"Not a chance," I say, and just that easily, Dash has me smiling when he kisses me goodbye and seals me in the hired SUV. But as the driver pulls us onto the road, I swear a bad feeling is clawing at me, and the past Allie, is suffocating me.

***

For most of the day, I expect to hear from Brandon, expect an explosion that doesn't come. As for my job, well, I don't resign. Mark is at the hospital with his mother all day so it's not exactly the right time to drop that bomb. I decide I wouldn't resign even if he was present today anyway. There's an idea brewing in my mind about how Hawk Legal and Riptide might become partners with me in a key role to win for both sides. But I need time to put those thoughts on paper and make sure everyone is as sold on the idea as I am.

I arrive back at the hotel to find Dash still at his computer. "How did writing go?"

"Damn good," he says. "I'm finally in a zone with this book." He stands and motions to the wine bottle on the coffee table.

We come together in the living room, and soon our glasses are filled, and when I would start asking questions about Brandon, he's already offering answers.

"No one at the publisher is calling Bella back about Brandon. I even tried to call, no one called me back."

My brows furrow. "They didn't call you? That feels weird, Dash."

"They're getting ready for the signing. I wouldn't read into it. How was your day at Riptide?"

"Good," I say. "And no, I didn't resign." I proceed to tell him my idea, that perhaps Hawk Legal could outsource their auctions to Riptide. "I could work on-site at Hawk Legal."

"You think they'll go for it?" he asks.

"I'm going to sell the hell out of it."

His cellphone rings and he glances at the caller ID. "That would be Bella." He answers the line on speaker. "You're on speaker, Bella. I'm with Allie."

"You're both about to lose your shit."

"What the hell does that mean, Bella?" Dash demands.

"Yes, what does that mean?" I ask, setting my glass down and turning toward Dash and the phone.

"Brandon is now repping—God, I can barely say it—your father, Dash."

"Oh my God," I say. "He went after someone close to Dash with the intent to hurt me by hurting him. I know he did. I *know* he did."

"Okay, this gets worse," she says. "A few hours ago, I asked for the promotional material for the signing because I just couldn't get a copy. I got irritated. I raised hell. They sent it to me."

"Just tell me what the hell is going on, Bella," Dash snaps.

"Apparently, Brandon set-up a Halloween signing for your father, Dash. Brandon swears he thought your father was the only one signing, but from talking to the publisher, they believed it was a father-son event. Something never done before."

"Holy fuck. Are you telling me I'm signing with my dad?"

"Yeah. And he's not happy about it either. But the publisher and the charity sent out a huge press blitz for this event just today, Dash. And yes, Brandon pushed for the blitz. You can't get out of this. And neither can he. And for the record, I talked to that prick Brandon myself. I called him myself. He knew exactly what he was doing. He knows you two don't speak, but apparently, he got your dad so much money, he feels like he'll forgive him this error. I'm going to get on a plane—"

"No," Dash says. "Stay there. It's a signing. It's complicated enough, Bella. And we both know this is too personal for both of us. I need you to keep your space and professionalism in case I don't."

"You have to, Dash," she insists. "This is really high-profile. And you'll have to take photos with him. I'm sorry. I wish I could make this go away. But believe you me, if I can make Brandon go away, I will. I'm going to report him to the ethics committee. He should not be an agent."

"I'll handle Brandon," Dash says. "Stay away from him. I want him to come for me, and only me. I'll call you tomorrow."

"Dash—"

"Later, Bella," he says, and he hangs up, setting the phone down.

"Dash, I'm so sorry," I say quickly. "This is because of me. If I'd told you about Brandon before now, maybe we could have—"

"No. No one could see this shit coming, Allie. You didn't do this. This isn't about you. It's about a couple of assholes. Your ex and my father." He stands up and walks to the patio doors, opening them and stepping outside in the bitter cold night, with no coat on.

I grab my own jacket and pull it on, following him outside. He's standing at the railing, holding onto the steel bars, face pointed skyward. I step to his side, shivering in the long moment that passes before Dash grabs me and pulls me in front of him.

My back is to the railing, his hands on my waist as he says, "Do not talk to my father. I need you to promise me you'll stay away from him."

I could be offended. I could get defensive. But I don't. This isn't about me and Dash. This is about Dash and his father. There's something between them, something he doesn't want me to be involved with. Something I can't push him to explain while he's dealing with this.

"Okay," I say. "I won't talk to your father."

"*Promise me*, Allie. Stay away from him."

"Yes, I promise. I'll stay away—"

Already his hand is in my hair, fingers twining roughly, his mouth claiming my mouth. He devours me with that kiss, anger burning on his tongue that has everything to do with his father and nothing to do with me. He tears his mouth from my mouth, and turns me to the railing. He drags my coat down my arms and throws it away, but I'm no longer cold. My hands are on the steel railings now and my skirt is at my waist. He yanks my panties and I gasp into the night, the mist of warm air fanning from my mouth.

Then Dash's fingers are between my legs, stroking me, teasing me, but the tease doesn't last long. I'm wet and ready, and he needs no further invitation. He drives into me, his hand smacking my backside, harder than I expect, but something arousing in a way I also do not expect, before he thrusts yet again.

There's a part of me then that knows that this is a time when Dash would fight, when he would look for an outlet. *I'm* that outlet tonight. But he's holding back. With his secrets, and how he fucks me. I don't know all there is to know about this man. Because he thinks I'll hate him if I do. But I won't, and as I push against him as he thrusts inside me, I know that this, what we are doing right now, isn't enough for him.

If I don't find a way to break through to Dash, he'll fight again. And he'll shut me out when he does.

CHAPTER FORTY-SEVEN

Dash doesn't say another word about his father.

After that cold, sexy encounter on the hotel balcony, we go to the gym and he runs for an hour. After that, we go to the room and have sex again. We wake up and repeat. Sex. Gym. Sex. All of this is a better outlet than fighting or booze, which the latter doesn't seem to be a vice for Dash. Just as he didn't let Tyler drive Allison home drunk, he doesn't let us drive drunk either. For all his self-hate, Dash is an amazing, giving person. I'm baffled as to why his father wouldn't feel the same.

It's almost noon when we eat a light lunch in the room. Dash heads to the shower, and I call Bella, who's been texting with me since Dash ordered her to stay home.

"How is he?"

"Broody," I say. "Don't tell me details, it's his story to tell, but do you even know why they hate each other?"

"No. He doesn't talk about it, and that's saying a lot considering how close we are."

"Yes. And I'm glad for it, Bella. He needs you."

"He needs you, too. I want to come there, I want to help."

"He knows that. And that's enough. He wants to fly home after the signing anyway. He chartered a plane," I say, sharing the news Dash had shared with me before we ever went to bed last night.

"I think that might be a good idea. Call me after the signing. Or text me if you can't call."

"I will," I promise, and set my phone down, praying this signing isn't going to go as badly as I think it might.

***

Dash dresses for the signing in black jeans, a thin black sweater, and a jacket, that he pairs with his favorite black boots. He looks handsome, cool, and every bit the famous writer that he's become. I wear a downplayed black dress for a reason. This day is about Dash. My role is one of support, my attention, and everyone else's, will be on him.

The signing itself is at a hotel overlooking Battery Park, where the ocean views are second only to the direct line of sight that is the Statue of Liberty. And holy wow, there are people waiting to get into the hotel everywhere. "They have to be freezing."

"I have loyal fans," Dash says, glancing over at me. "But then, so does my father."

Not like Dash, I think, and I wonder if that's a problem between them, perhaps not "the" problem, but a problem.

Dash laces his fingers with mine. "Stay with me, even when I'm signing."

"I'll be right there," I promise, certain this attachment is about the other promise I made, to avoid his father.

The driver pulls us to a side entrance and security ushers us inside. A petite woman with dark hair and glasses, whose age I just can't name, greets us. Tina, as she tells us is her name, quickly declares herself Dash's ambassador. Ambassador of what, I don't know, but apparently making him comfortable because she guides us to a private room where there are chairs, water, a television, and snacks.

"Your father is one room over," she says. "Or he will be when he arrives. We'd planned on doing a little chat with both of you and the press before we opened the doors, but we'll have to run with that after the event.

He's running late. The guests are outside freezing their asses off so we will want to start right on time." She eyes her watch. "That's in half an hour. Can I get you anything now?"

"No," Dash says. "We're good."

Her phone buzzes with a message, she quickly reads before she says, "Dash, I just got word that the powers that be would like to go forward with the photo op and question-and-answer session without your father. Are you okay with that?"

"That's why I'm here," he says. "To do whatever I need to do to ensure the event is successful."

"I heard you were down to earth and really great to work with. I heard right. Give me five and I'll be back to get you.

She exits and Dash glances over at me. "Chicken shit is hiding."

"You don't think he'll no show, do you?"

"No. He'll come in the last minute to avoid being compared to me on stage, or better yet, asked about me being his pride and joy. He'd choke on the words."

I step to him and wrap my arms around him. "Well, I'm excited to experience this. I can't wait to see all the fans that love you almost as much as I do."

"You love me, huh?" he says, molding me closer.

"I do, Dash," I say, surprised at how easily those words roll off my tongue. "Very much."

"Say it again."

I laugh. "I love you, Dash Black."

"I love you, too, cupcake."

There's a knock on the door and Tina pokes her head inside. "We're a go."

Dash releases me and draws a breath, and gives Tina a wave of readiness. Turns out, the press and photo op are in a private room that is quite large. I sit in a row of what must be fifty seats, all filled with book and entertainment reporters.

Dash sits on a stage with someone named Alex and answers his questions, which range from his books to the movies, before Alex takes questions from the crowd. All the while, cameras flash, from all sides of the room. And all the while I wait anxiously, nervously, for Brandon or Dash's father to show up, or perhaps both.

When finally, Alex announces, "Nathan Black is in the house. And the crowds outside are ready for food, prizes, and signed books."

Dash stands and walks down the stairs, motioning for me to join him. He reaches for my hand and cameras flash. Someone calls out, "Who's your lady friend, Dash?" but Dash keeps walking.

We exit to a private hallway where Tina meets us. "They're opening the doors right now. We need to get you to your table." She motions for us to follow and hurries forward.

We enter a room lined with windows that open to a view that is ocean blue brilliance. The room itself is decorated with Halloween décor and there are little tables of cupcakes and finger foods.

"Thank fuck," Dash says, when he realizes his father's table is on the far side of the room. They literally cannot interact, nor can I interact with his father. I can't even really make out what he looks like from this distance. That's how big the room is. That's how far away he is. I don't think Brandon is here either. I guess he stirred the caldron with a little acid and then left us all to fall in. The problem is that Brandon isn't someone who leaves anything to chance.

Even if he's not here, he has a plan to make that acid burn.

CHAPTER FORTY-EIGHT

Dash sits down at his signing table and pulls a chair up for me beside him. I claim it eagerly and say, "I know how crazy signings can get. I'll help you manage the craziness. I love this, Dash. The readers. The books. Focus on this being your life, not your father."

"Good advice, cupcake. Good advice."

And no sooner than he says those words, the doors open and the crowds rush forward, security guards forming lines. Before long, Dash and I are talking to his fans, and he's not the only one in the pictures. I'm with him so the fans want shots of me, as well. It's kind of silly but I go with the flow. Time ticks on and the lines don't ease, but Dash's father's line is not anywhere near as long as his. I feel a pinch of discomfort for him. I mean, it has to be hard to be second best, but then again, shouldn't a parent have pride in their child?

Dash's ex-editor, Ellen, checks on him several times, giving me a side-eye as she does. Guess she knows I get to read his books first now. I kind of can't help but get a thrill from that after she had me edit his book and took the credit way back when.

Hours pass, and the crowd disperses. Tina reappears and kneels between us. "I want to get you and your dad in a few photos, Dash."

I glance over at his father's table and he's already left the signing area, which I can assume means he's already at the photo op. Dash isn't getting out of direct contact with him, but then neither is his father with him.

Tina's phone buzzes with a text and she glances at it before saying, "Okay, I need to talk to security. I'll meet you in the hallway." She hurries away.

I rotate to face Dash, my hand on his leg. "Just do it and get it over with. Take the photos. Say nothing. Come back to me."

He stands and pulls me to my feet. "I need you to wait in the holding room, Allie."

"Dash—"

He presses his hand to my shoulder. "Please."

My belly flutters with worry and I reluctantly say, "Yes. Okay."

He laces the fingers of one hand with his and starts walking. He doesn't stop until I'm in that holding room.

"This will be fast." That's all he says, and then he's gone, exiting the room and shutting the door. I start to pace, fretting over what could go wrong. If either of them shows animosity with each other, they'll be all over the internet. But I'm only pacing five minutes when the door opens and Dash reappears.

"He's not feeling well," Dash announces of his father. "No photo op. We are free to get the hell out of here."

"Oh good. Yes. Now. Please."

Dash already has my hand in his and we're walking down the hallway, toward the exit. "The driver's waiting on us."

We're almost to the door when I spy a bathroom. "I have to stop. We've been at that table for hours."

"Yeah. Not a bad idea, especially since there's apparently a traffic jam we have to make it through to get back to the hotel."

"I'll be fast," I say, darting into the bathroom. And I am fast, so fast, but not fast enough.

I step into the hallway to find Dash and his father standing toe-to-toe. I inhale and step to Dash's side. His father, who resembles Dash, but with gray hair, his stature less potent, his skin a bit too sun-kissed, jerks his gaze to me.

"Does she know who you really are?" he demands, as if I'm not here, as if he's not looking right at me.

"Go to the car, Allie," Dash orders.

"Why?" his father demands. "So she won't hear you're a killer? So she won't know you were with your brother when he died?"

"I wasn't with him when he died. Allie—"

"You let him die."

"I was not his damn keeper," Dash snaps.

"Piece of shit. You don't deserve your success. Sounds like you made a deal with the devil to me."

My God, I think. The way he's talking to Dash. "Let's go, Dash," I say, tugging his arm. "Let's go now."

His father looks at me again. "He'll hurt you. Maybe you'll accidentally end up dead, like my son."

"*He's* your son, too," I snap at him. "Then again, you're no father. Come now, Dash."

Dash stares at his father another beat and then turns and starts walking, taking me with him, but I'm a willing companion. Security opens the door for us and we climb into the back of the SUV.

"Drive," Dash orders the minute he shuts the door.

The driver sets us in motion, but Dash doesn't look at me. He lowers his head, fingers tunneling into his hair. I want to touch him. I want to talk to him, but I know we're not alone and he's a hair away from snapping. And he does. Suddenly, he looks up and says, "Stop the vehicle."

I turn to him. "What? Why?"

The driver pulls us to a sidewalk and Dash opens the door and gets out. I follow him, but he catches my arms and halts me at the door.

"We don't work. I was selfish to think we worked, Allie. Go home. It's better that way. Neil will watch over you until this Allison thing is figured out. He'll call you. Answer when he does."

My eyes burn and my chest pinches. "Don't do this," I plead. "Don't let him blaming you for something that wasn't your fault divide us."

"How do you know it wasn't my fault, Allie? How do you know anything about me when you don't know that?"

"Don't go and fight, Dash. Brandon, and your father, they're watching. This was all planned. They want to take you down. Don't fight. Please. I'm begging you."

"Go home," he says again, and with that bitter command, he releases me, and turns, and starts walking. I round the door and intend to follow, and I try, but I make it half a block and he's just gone. I can't see him anymore.

I'm trembling when I climb back into the SUV and shut the door. "Where to, ma'am?"

Where to?

Home, Dash said. I don't even know where that is right now, but obviously, Dash just broke up with me. I give the driver my apartment address. I sink back into the seat and try to breathe and calm myself. I will not melt down here, right now. I won't. And somehow, I really do hold it together. I arrive at my apartment and dig in my purse, thankful I always keep a key in my side pocket, just in case. I'm still trembling, so much so that I can barely open my door. I flip on the light and just stare at the familiar space. My apartment. I lock up and walk to the bedroom, sitting on the mattress and plopping my purse on the bed next to me.

Now, the tears flow. Now, they stream down my cheeks. Maybe this really is where I belong after all.

THE END...FOR NOW

BECAUSE I CAN

The finale for the Necklace Trilogy will be out next month!! Get it here:

https://www.lisareneejones.com/necklace-trilogy.html

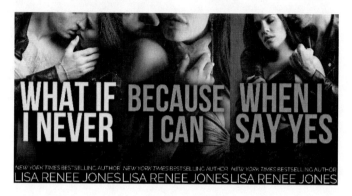

***

Don't forget, if you want to be the first to know about upcoming books, giveaways, sales, and any other exciting news I have to share please be sure you're signed up for my newsletter! As an added bonus everyone receives a free eBook when they sign-up!

http://lisareneejones.com/newsletter-sign-up/

***

Don't miss the Lucifer Trilogy coming soon—the latest Walker Security series!

LISA RENEE JONES

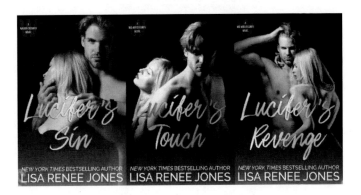

https://www.lisareneejones.com/walker-security-lucifers-trilogy.html

EXCERPT FROM THE WALKER SECURITY: ADRIAN TRILOGY

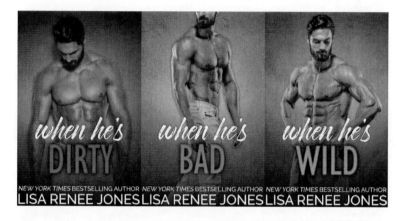

I exit the bathroom and halt to find him standing in the doorway, his hands on either side of the doorframe. "What are you doing?

"This," he says, and suddenly, his hands are on my waist, and he's walked me back into the bathroom.

Before I know what's happening, he's kicked the door shut, and his fingers are diving into my hair. "Kissing you, because I can't fucking help myself. And because you might not ever let me do it again. That is unless you object?"

That's the part that really gets me. The "unless I object," the way he manages to be all alpha and demanding and still ask. Well, and the part where he can't fucking help himself.

I press to my toes and the minute my mouth meets his, his crashes over mine, his tongue doing a wicked lick that I feel in every part of me. And I don't know what I taste like to him, but he is temptation with a hint of tequila, demand, and desire. His hands slide up my back, fingers splayed between my shoulder blades, his hard body pressed to mine, seducing me in every possible way.

I moan with the feel of him and his lips part from mine, lingering there a moment before he says, "Obviously, someone needs to protect you from me," he says. "Like me." And then to my shock, he releases me and leaves. The bathroom door is open and closed before I know what's happened. And once again, I have no idea if or when I will ever see him again.

FIND OUT MORE ABOUT THE ADRIAN TRILOGY HERE:

https://www.lisareneejones.com/walker-security-adrians-trilogy.html

GET A FREE COPY OF BOOK ONE HERE:

https://claims.prolificworks.com/free/I3n4VacJ

THE BRILLIANCE TRILOGY

It all started with a note, just a simple note handwritten by a woman I didn't know, never even met. But in that note is perhaps every answer to every question I've ever had in my life. And because of that note, I look for her but find him. I'm drawn to his passion, his talent, a darkness in him that somehow becomes my light, my life. Kace August is rich, powerful, a rock star of violins, a man who is all tattoos, leather, good looks, and talent. He has a wickedly sweet ability to play the violin, seducing audiences worldwide. Now, he's seducing me. I know he has secrets. I don't care. Because you see, I have secrets, too.

I'm not Aria Alard, as he believes. I'm Aria Stradivari, daughter to Alessandro Stradivari, a musician born from the same blood as the man who created the famous Stradivarius violin. I am as rare as the mere 650 instruments my ancestors created. Instruments worth millions. 650 masterpieces, the brilliance unmatched.

650 reasons to kill. 650 reasons to hide. One reason not to: him.

FIND OUT MORE ABOUT THE BRILLIANCE TRILOGY HERE:

https://www.lisareneejones.com/brilliance-trilogy.html

GET A FREE COPY OF BOOK ONE HERE:

https://claims.prolificworks.com/free/FTpzSTRe

THE LILAH LOVE SERIES

As an FBI profiler, it's Lilah Love's job to think like a killer. And she is very good at her job. When a series of murders surface—the victims all stripped naked and shot in the head—Lilah's instincts tell her it's the work of an assassin, not a serial killer. But when the case takes her back to her hometown in the Hamptons and a mysterious but unmistakable connection to her own life, all her assumptions are shaken to the core.

Thrust into a troubled past she's tried to shut the door on, Lilah's back in the town where her father is mayor, her brother is police chief, and she has an intimate history with the local crime lord's son, Kane Mendez. The two share a devastating secret, and only

Kane understands Lilah's own darkest impulses. As more corpses surface, so does a series of anonymous notes to Lilah, threatening to expose her. Is the killer someone in her own circle? And is she the next target?

FIND OUT MORE ABOUT THE LILAH LOVE SERIES HERE:

https://www.lisareneejonesthrillers.com/the-lilah-love-series.html

ALSO BY LISA RENEE JONES

THE INSIDE OUT SERIES

If I Were You
Being Me
Revealing Us
*His Secrets**
Rebecca's Lost Journals
*The Master Undone**
*My Hunger**
No In Between
*My Control**
I Belong to You
*All of Me**

THE SECRET LIFE OF AMY BENSEN

Escaping Reality
Infinite Possibilities
Forsaken
*Unbroken**

CARELESS WHISPERS

Denial
Demand
Surrender

WHITE LIES

Provocative
Shameless

TALL, DARK & DEADLY

Hot Secrets
Dangerous Secrets
Beneath the Secrets

WALKER SECURITY

Deep Under
Pulled Under
Falling Under

LILAH LOVE

Murder Notes
Murder Girl
Love Me Dead
Love Kills
Bloody Vows
Bloody Love
Happy Death Day
The Party's Over

DIRTY RICH

Dirty Rich One Night Stand
Dirty Rich Cinderella Story
Dirty Rich Obsession
Dirty Rich Betrayal
Dirty Rich Cinderella Story: Ever After
Dirty Rich One Night Stand: Two Years Later
Dirty Rich Obsession: All Mine
Dirty Rich Secrets
Dirty Rich Betrayal: Love Me Forever

THE FILTHY TRILOGY

The Bastard
The Princess
The Empire

THE NAKED TRILOGY

One Man
One Woman
Two Together

THE SAVAGE SERIES

Savage Hunger
Savage Burn
Savage Love
Savage Ending

THE BRILLIANCE TRILOGY

A Reckless Note
A Wicked Song
A Sinful Encore

ADRIAN'S TRILOGY

When He's Dirty
When He's Bad
When He's Wild

NECKLACE TRILOGY

What If I Never?
Because I Can
When I Say Yes

*eBook only

ABOUT LISA RENEE JONES

New York Times and *USA Today* bestselling author Lisa Renee Jones writes dark, edgy fiction including the highly acclaimed *Inside Out* series and the crime thriller *The Poet*. Suzanne Todd (producer of Alice in Wonderland and Bad Moms) on the *Inside Out* series: *Lisa has created a beautiful, complicated, and sensual world that is filled with intrigue and suspense.*

Prior to publishing, Lisa owned a multi-state staffing agency that was recognized many times by The Austin Business Journal and also praised by the Dallas Women's Magazine. In 1998 Lisa was listed as the #7 growing women-owned business in Entrepreneur Magazine. She lives in Colorado with her husband, a cat that talks too much, and a Golden Retriever who is afraid of trash bags.

Made in United States
North Haven, CT
21 January 2022

15058729R00131